Boy, I Had Enough!

A Novel by

Terry L. Wroten

ISBN 978-9834573-3-6

Chapter 1

Daphne

I was fourteen when I fell in love with my baby daddy. His name is Charlie. I met Charlie at the Crenshaw Mall while I was out shopping with two of my homegirls, Monica and Mo'nique. We were walking out of Lady Footlocker when Charlie and his best friend, Maine, emerged out of nowhere.

I had on some Gucci shoes and tight Gucci blue jeans with a Gucci tank top. Mya and Mo'nique had on the same thing. We were taking pictures that day, and dressed like triplets. Both of my homegirls were some dimes, but I considered myself the prettiest. I stood five foot seven and had a body like Beyonce. My hair was wavy and long. It's jet black and matches perfectly with my golden bronze complexion. My eyes are hazel, so most people think I'm mixed. I have a little Blackfoot Indian in me, that's about it. Other than that, both of my parents are black.

Now, Mya and Mo'nique are sisters. They're both from the projects. They both have nice features, but Mya is caramel and Mo'nique is chocolate. Mya is petite and Mo'nique is thick. They're both five foot five.

As we walked out of Lady Footlocker, we smack into two guys.

"Damn, where y'all come from? God must have sent y'all from the heavens above." One of the guys said as he reached down to pick up my purse, which I had dropped when we collided.

This boy couldn't be much older than me, and he was spitting game like a grown man. He was cute, and I was loving the attention, so I blushed and replied, "He sho' has, because we know we some angels."

"Well, if y'all some angels, won't y'all come save me and my boy? I'm Charlie, and this is my boy, Maine. We are some sinners, and we need some angels like y'all to guide us straight."

"That's real." Maine added.

I looked Charlie and his boy over. They both stood roughly five foot eleven. Charlie was about 180lbs, and Maine was about five pounds lighter than him. Charlie's complexion is copper-brown, and Maine's skin tone is dukey brown. They both had short cut hairdos. They rated an eight on the beauty scale of 1 to 10. I knew from their gear and car keys that they had money. The car keys were to a Benz.

Mo'nique was the more outgoing sister. She said, "I see y'all dressed to impress, so where y'all from?"

Maine replied, "We from where y'all want us to be from. Naw, for real, we from Queens."

"The East Coast!" Charlie added proudly.

Upon hearing the East Coast, the first thing that came to mind was, *they Crips*. In Los Angeles, if you tell a nigga from the hood that you from the East Coast, they'll automatically assume you are a Crip. One of the biggest Crip sects in Los Angeles are the East Coast Crips, so I immediately thought Charlie and Maine were East Coast Crip gang members.

One thing I knew for sure was that the East Coast Crips hung on the east side of LA, so I asked, "Y'all some eastside niggas, huh?"

Charlie replied, "Yo, hol' on shawty. Don't get us twisted with that fuckery. We're not from East Coast Crips. We from the East Coast, East Coast!"

Maine added, "The N-Y. Queens, New York!"

I smiled. Charlie and Maine were some out of state niggas, fresh meat to my young mind. "What y'all doin' out here?" I wanted to know.

Charlie chuckled. "Ma, you're askin' a lotta questions, you must be interested."

Charlie was too blunt for my taste. I was only fourteen and not as street smart as I pretended to be. I forced a smile and fumbled with my words. "If-If I wasn't interested, I wouldn't be wasting my time."

That was all it took. I gave Charlie my number and Mo'nique gave Maine hers.

As we walked off, Mya said, "Y'all just give y'all numbers to anybody. Y'all easy…"

Later that night, I sat at the dinner table with my parents. My father was a conservative man, and he enforced strict rules on me. I could not do any of the things most fourteen year-old girls did, so I had to be real sneaky and rebellious at times. My father was a commercial general contractor, so he traveled the world. With his job keeping him away ten to twenty days out of the month, I was only locked down a week or two at a time.

My mother was a public school teacher, so she was passive to some of the things I did, like going to the mall or to the movies with my friends. However, my father was the one who stayed on me like white on rice. When it came to him, a bitch couldn't do shit. He didn't tolerate me doing nothing. I couldn't even go to the projects I grew up in to hang with Mya and Mo'nique. And his biggest no-no was boys calling the house. To him, I grown and living on my own, so I couldn't date or even wave at a boy, let alone have a boy call his place of residence asking for me.

When my father was promoted to department head of the Fortune 500 Company he worked for, he moved me and my mother out of the ghetto and told us he don't ever want us to go back. I understood that the Nicholson Gardens Housing Projects in Watts were deadly, but I didn't understand why my father would restrict my mother and I from going to the projects, when we still had family and friends there. I never questioned my father's authority, so I never found out why.

On this night, after I gave Charlie my number and told my father I'd been down the street all day at my white friend, Carol's house, I got busted.

As my parents and I sat eating fried chicken and mashed potatoes, the phone went off. I knew nine times out of ten it was for me, because my father stayed away from home on business, and my mother barely talked on the phone. She stayed busy correcting papers and grading homework. I was the phone junky. On most days after school, I'd find myself caught up on the phone with either Mya, Mo'nique or the party line.

I leapt from my seat on the second ring to answer the phone, but my father said, "I got it."

The kitchen phone was on the wall and in arms reach from where he was seated. He reached over and hit the speaker button.

"Hello!"

"Hello! Is Daphne home?"

"Who's callin'?" my father immediately asked.

"Charles."

"Daddy, I got it." I said.

Charlie had called at the wrong damn time.

My father looked at me and snarled, "No. I got it!"

I looked at my mother and she stayed quiet. I wanted her to say, "Darryl, just let the girl talk," but she didn't. I sat back down at the table and my father asked Charlie where he knew me from.

Charlie replied, "Yo, I don't want any problems. I just met Daphne today at the mall. Shawty was with her homegirls and I was with my man."

My father's whole demeanor changed. "Aye, bruh! I don't know how old you are, but Daphne is only fourteen. I don't allow her to talk on the phone, so don't call here no more!"

Charlie said, "Alright," and hung up.

I was tired of my father's rules and bullshit, and he was tired of me messing up.

"Daddy, you didn't have to do dat."

My mother knew my father was going to snap from my comment. "Daphne, you know boys are not allowed to be call here, so go to your room before your father goes off."

I couldn't hold back anymore. I was growing tired of my father's strictness and his fucked up attitude.

"I feel like a prisoner of war in this house. I can't do anything! I can't even breathe without y'all trippin'," I hissed.

"Well, if you don't like my rules, get out! Then you could make your own rules!" My father sounded like James Earl Jones. He frequently told me and my mother to get out when things weren't going his way. I actually hated my father. He treated me and my mother like shit. He had over ten different baby mommas, and my mother was the only one who was stupid enough to put up with his shit.

However, I wasn't going to keep letting him treat me like a prisoner. I said, "Well, I guess, that's what I gotta do, because I'm outta here."

I ran to my room, grabbed some outfits, and walked to the door. My mother begged me to stay. She was too scared to leave my father, but I wasn't! I said, "Momma, when you gain enough strength to leave your womanizer then I'll stay with you. Other than that, I'd rather live life on my own and as it comes."

Two hours later, I was in the projects. Mya and Mo'nique had let me come stay with them, but Junie, their cracked head mom, was talking about I had to pay to stay, and I wasn't even in that filthy apartment thirty minutes. I was contemplating going around the corner to my Aunt Michelle's unit, but she was an alcoholic. She was worse than Junie.

After I sat on Mo'nique's bed for forty minutes contemplating my next move, I decided to call Charlie to let him know how it was all his fault I got kicked out of my house. I grabbed the house phone off Monica's nightstand and told Mo'nique my plan.

"Shit, if the nigga any good, he probably could help us out."

Mo'nique and I were in the same boat. She wanted so badly to get away from her mother. She hated the way Junie neglected her and her sister. Mya didn't care what their mother did. She wasn't fast like Mo'nique and I. She was all about school and running track. At fifteen years old, she had me and Mo'nique by a year. Mo'nique and I were closer because we were more street oriented than Monica.

"Yep. If the nigga any good, he sho' can help us," I replied.

"But, Daphne, you know most niggas want somthin' in return when they do somethin' for you."

Mo'nique was right. I knew that was the truth, so I decided not to call Charlie. I was still a virgin and didn't know what Charlie would think if I told him I wasn't educated down there like that. I knew from the way I immediately saw dollar signs on him that other girls saw the same dollar signs and threw their panties at him.

"Yeah, you right!" I told Mo'nique. "I can't just give myself up that easy. Matter of fact, I don't even wanna call his New York ass no more."

"Shit, I don't know why not," Mo'nique replied. "You're gonna lose yo' virginity one day. Plus, if you don't wanna be in this filthy-ass apartment or yo' aunt's house, you gotta do somethin'."

Again, Mo'nique had a point. She had lost her virginity at age twelve, so she moved a little faster than

I did in that area. We sat talking for about another hour and I let her talk me into calling Charlie.

Chapter 2

Charlie

I was thinking about the big booty cutie I'd met at the mall earlier that day as I hopped out of my Benz and got into my 2002 Denali. I couldn't get Daphne off my mind. After dropping off a package at the post office for express mail, I was on my way to meet my boy, Maine, at our new apartment complex we'd just purchased in Hawthorne, California.

My phone went off and I looked at my Nextel. It was Maine. I didn't have to answer, because he put in our code to let me know he was waiting for me at the apartment complex. I was already in Inglewood, the neighboring city to Hawthorne, so I tossed my cell phone back on the passenger seat.

I was on 104th Street and Yukon when Daphne popped back in my head. I was mad at myself because I vowed never to mess with another Cali girl. My first Cali girlfriend/baby momma Shondella had caused so much drama in my life, I didn't need another Cali problem. And just as I told myself Cali girls are too much drama, I bumped into Daphne.

Daphne and her homegirl, Mo'nique, were so thick my dick jumped out of my pants when I noticed them. Off top, I envisioned myself fucking them at the same time. It was just my fantasy to have two thick Cali girls in bed together. However, looks could be deceiving. I thought Daphne and Mo'nique were at least twenty, until they told me they both were sixteen. Then, come to find out, Daphne was only fourteen, and I was three years older than her.

When I made it to 134th Street and Yukon, I parked in front of my apartment complex and smiled. Maine and I were probably the youngest East Coast dudes to come to Cali and have it our way. At seventeen, we owned ten cars and ten trucks combined, and three apartment buildings. Two in Queens, and this new one in Hawthorne. Since we were barely making our names known on the West Coast, we only kept two of our vehicles in Cali.

I hopped out of my truck and my two Crip homies, Peewee and Black Dice, hopped out of their cars. I associated with Crips and Bloods in Cali, and they all respected my hustle. We greeted, and Peewee said, "Yo son, what's the deal, kid?"

I laughed. Peewee stayed mimicking our style of speech on the East Coast. I took him and Black Dice to Harlem with me one time, and he quickly picked up the lingo. They went with me because they were from a gang called Harlem Crips. There were Harlem Crips in Harlem, New York, but Peewee and Black Dice were from the LA chapter, and they were my West Coast gunners. They were with anything that was going to put money in their pockets.

My baby momma, Maria, was Puerto Rican, and her brothers put a hit out on me because I impregnated their sister and left her crazy ass. I was fifteen when I had my twins by Maria, and she was twenty. I took Peewee and Black Dice out there with me, and they did some straight up South Central shoot 'em up bang-bang type shit. Now, I got Harlem on lock. However, I stay away from Harlem, because Maria suspects I had her brothers killed and she wants to kill me.

Due to all the baby momma drama with Maria, I shipped supplies to my Harlem lieutenant, Gotti, and he took care of the twins for me. At seventeen, I had five kids and one on the way. Charlene, in Atlanta was seven months pregnant, and she was already talking about child support. My brother and Maine stayed warning me about using protection, but I was too young and too dumb to listen. My alias was Bare Back King when it came to females, because I was known to fuck them raw dog.

I replied to Peewee's greeting and said, "Cuzz, it's not what's the deal. It's what's crackin' fo da nite?"

Peewee laughed and gave me dap. Black Dice never did too much talking, so I nodded 'Wassup' to him and he nodded back.

We walked to the last apartment in my ten unit apartment complex. Maine opened the door and said, "Aiyo money, we got some strippas in here tonight, courtesy of Bull and Bunch."

Bull and Bunch were my two Blood homeboys. They were also part of the West Coast team. My team on the

West Coast hung out with each other on the money tip, so there was never a Blood and Crip issue between them. And what made the crew so wicked, we were all seventeen and eighteen and hungry for money and pussy.

When we walked in, Peewee and Black Dice greeted their would be enemies with hugs. Maine turned down the music and told the five strippers it was time to get the party started.

I didn't even notice the five strippers sitting and standing around our kitchen table until Maine turned down the music. Two of them were Asians, one Latina, and two sisters, a red bone and a chocolate.

I've never discriminated on a female because of her ethnicity, but I love my dark women; the darker the berry, the sweeter the juice. Before the strippers started doing their thing, I motioned for the chocolate one to come over. As she walked toward the entrance where I was standing, I realized she had a body of a goddess and her face wasn't from hell. It was at least an eight on the scale of beauty.

Off top, I recognized a flaw in her. It was a major turn off seeing a woman smoke. When I saw a cigarette dangling between her fingers and a blunt sitting on her left ear, I damn near told her to get out. However, when she approached and said, “Hi,” I became fascinated with her teeth and smile. I love a woman with nice pearly whites and a beautiful smile. In addition to that, her blue Guess jeans were complimenting her every curve. My dick was jumping for joy.

“Look, ma, take that blunt from yo’ ear and throw that cigarette away. And when you’re done, meet me in the back room.” I pointed to the back room to show her what room I was talking about. There were three bedrooms in the apartment.

My team realized what I was doing and started laughing.

Maine said, “Yo, wear a rain coat, B.”

I chuckled and threw up the peace sign as I walked off.

In the back room, I sat on the king size bed I never used. Chocolate sat next to me with her hand on my thigh. She was ready to go to work, and said, “Look, I don’t normally do private one on ones unless I’m gettin’ two gees or more, but I see you’re a young stunna. You could give me five hundred for the whole package.”

I looked Chocolate up and down and laughed. "Ma, you don't gotta give me no discount. I pay in full for services I receive. But right now, I didn't bring you back here to get in yo' pants. We can do that later. At this very moment, I wanna pick yo' brain."

I operated on the motto, 'business before pleasure,' so I started in on my questions.

"Aiyo, ma, how much do you get paid in one night? How many hours do you work? Do you love yo' J-O-B? Do you have an out plan? Do you have any kids? How much is yo' monthly rent and car note? Do you have a boyfriend? What's the last grade you completed? Do you like traveling? Do you have any family outside of Cali?"

I fired the questions of quickly, not giving her a chance to even respond. I wanted to test her memory and attention to detail.

She didn't disappoint, only one or two minor inquiries were missed in her rapid fire answer. After I picked Chocolate's brain, I found out that she was the youngest of six. Her government was Janet Gibbs, and her dancing name was X-tasy, but I nicknamed her Chocolate. On an average day of dancing, she made close to $500 a night. She stripped to support herself, her four-year-old son, and her eighteen-year-old sister. She was twenty-two and dropped out of college her freshman year after giving birth to her son. She was single, enjoyed traveling, and had family in Spokane, Washington. She stayed in Los Angeles and her monthly cost of living ranged from $1500 to $3000.

I was on top of my game and decided not to stick my dick in Chocolate. I needed to employ her. After I gave her my cell number and told her to call me in the morning, I reached in my pocket and pulled out $5000 and told her not to ask any questions.

After she grabbed the money, I dismissed her.

She grabbed my hand and said, "Damn, you don't want no ass? What, I'm not good enough for you?"

Chocolate didn't know what I had planned for her, so I countered, "Don't trip! Ma, I want more than just ass. I like you as a woman, so I'm not gonna treat you like a hoe. See, after you walk out this room, I'ma call one of them Asian bitches and fuck her hard."

I slipped up and said the wrong thing. I knew better than to tell a black woman that I'd rather have sex with another woman from another race than her. Chocolate snapped, but she tried not to show it. Her demeanor told me I messed up, so I gave in.

"Look, shawty, since you wanna give me some ass, you gotta go all out. I want you to put it on me."

Chocolate smiled triumphantly. "I don't think that's a lot to ask, but do you have a condom? Because I'm very fertile and don't need any more kids."

I shook my head. Chocolate was a blunt broad, however, I was the Bare Back King. Condoms were something I didn't carry. I told Chocolate I don't normally trick off my John, so I don't keep condoms on me.

"Well, I got a few Magnums in my purse."

I was damned. I hated condoms. They took away from the pleasure. Plus, I thought I was too good to catch any disease or virus.

Chocolate's purse was in the kitchen, so she excused herself to go and get it. As she walked out, my cell phone went off. It was a little after midnight, so I knew it was one of my West Coast business partners. On the East Coast, it was about three in the morning.

I looked at the area code and it was a 323 number. *LA* I thought. *Damn, who could dis be?* I almost didn't answer, because I didn't know who the call was coming from. However, I flipped open my phone and it was Daphne.

"Charlie, you got me kicked outta my house," she said before I could even say hello.

I wanted to laugh in her face, but I kept my laugh in. Daphne was kicked out of her house because she lied to me. If she would have told me her real age, I wouldn't have called her house, especially not her father's crib. However, I felt bad. I knew the game, and I was supposed to have hung up when a man answered the phone.

"Shawty, you brought all dis on yo' self. If you woulda kept it real, I wouldn't have called ya pop's house like dat."

"Well, I thought if I told you my real age, you woulda lost interest. But if I'm too young for you, I understand."

At that moment, Chocolate walked back into the room smiling and holding up three Magnums. I whispered, "Hol' on." I didn't want to just hang up on Daphne, so I told her to call me back in exactly an hour.

She said, "Okay," and I hung up.

When I hung up, Chocolate said, "That must have been a booty call."

I chuckled. "Naw, ma, that was business. I'ma businessman."

I thought about my own statement and laughed. I was very business minded. Daphne called right on time. I had four empty apartments and planned to give her and Chocolate one. However, as I thought about my next move, Chocolate started stripping me out of my clothes. My John immediately rose like yeast.

Chocolate just took charge. She stripped me out of my clothes, put a Magnum on my dick, bent over, reached between her legs, grabbed my dick, and put it in her womb. It was warm, tight, and gushy. I grabbed her ass and started pounding away.

Chocolate was a freak. She started oohing and aahing. Her moans made me pound like a mad man. She moaned, "Faster." I started pounding harder and faster. The harder and faster I pumped, the louder she became.

I was fucking the shit out of Chocolate from the back. She was loving every bit of pipe I was laying. But as soon as I started deep stroking her, the condom broke. I slowed down to a stop and Chocolate moaned, "Please, don't stop."

That was music to my ears. I was the Bare Back King; she didn't have to ask me twice. I kept at it until we exploded. After I felt my fluids enter her womb, I snapped out of my spell and blurted, "Damn!"

"What's wrong?" Chocolate asked.

"Nothing."

She then dropped to her knees and started twirling her tongue around the head of my dick. I lay in bed with my hands behind my head and my legs spread eagle like a dead cockroach. Chocolate licked on my dick until it got hard again. When I was back hard as a rock, she jumped on top of me without protection and rode me like a jockey.

My phone went off right after we got dressed. It was Daphne. I told Chocolate to go wash up and wait for me in the living room. I talked on the phone with Daphne for an hour and she told me everything. She told me her father was a control freak, she was a virgin, mo'nique's mother was a crackhead, and they both wanted to leave home.

I ended up telling her and Mo'nique to pack all their belongings and I'll pick them up from Watts in the morning. When I hung up with Daphne, I walked back into the living room. All the strippers were smoking and drinking.

"Aiyo, whatchu do, fall in love? Whatchu tell her, don't strip fo' us out here? Because ma just came in here and said she's only waitin' on you."

I smiled inwardly. My boy Maine was a fool. We grew up together, so he knew me like the back of his hand.

I told him the plan for Chocolate, Daphne, and Mo'nique and he gave me some dap. "My dude, you're a genius."

I looked over at Bull, Bunch, Peewee, and Black Dice. They were all in their own little world. They stayed having what I called their West Coast Swag going on. With big Kush blunts and bottles of Remy in rotation, they stayed tipsy.

As they sat buzzed and mingling with the other strippers, I grabbed Chocolate by the arm and escorted her to the bathroom. I had to cleanse myself, so I decided to test her loyalty. Chocolate ended up cleaning me from head to toe, and as she cleaned me, I laced her with the game.

She agreed to ride with me 'til the wheels fell off. I agreed to take care of her, her son, and her sister. This was the beginning of a long journey.

Chapter 3

Daphne

That night, I called Charlie, and he came to pick me and Mo'nique up the next morning. When he arrived in the projects, all the Blood gang members who ran the projects envied him. I even mumbled, "Damn," to myself. Charlie was driving a pearl white Denali truck on 20-inch rims. He was bumping one of Nas' songs. Behind him, Maine was driving a jet black Benz with rims on it. They both had two passengers. The two that rolled with Charlie were Crips. Their names were Peewee and Black Dice. The other two that rolled with Maine were Bloods, which surprised me. Charlie had two Bloods and two Crips hanging together. The two Bloods were Bull and Bunch. They were from Brimz.

When Charlie pulled up, Bull and Bunch immediately hopped out of Maine's Benz. They walked directly over to the Bloods who ran the projects and started shaking their hands. I guess they went to introduce themselves and let the other Bloods know that Charlie was cool.

As Bull and Bunch stood across the street talking to the other Bloods, Charlie and Maine hopped out of their vehicles and helped me and Mo'nique load our stuff. We didn't have much, so they hopped out just to flaunt.

Peewee and Black Dice sat in the Denali observing everything. I knew they knew, they were in the wrong territory, but I didn't see their guns sitting in their laps until I loaded my three bags of clothes into the truck and hopped in. With the guns they had, I knew, they were killers.

After Mo'nique loaded all her belongings in Maine's Benz and Bull and Bunch finished talking to the other Bloods, we drove off. Mo'nique rolled with Maine because he was trying to holla at her. I rolled in the passenger seat of Charlie's truck. Peewee, who was in the passenger when Charlie rolled up, let me take shotgun.

He said, "I know you wanna sit in the front, so get yo' thick ass up here."

Peewee was shorter than me. He stood about five foot two. He had that flashy California look; clearly, he considered himself a gangsta and a pretty boy. He had wavy hair and was the same complexion as Charlie. He was also very talkative, unlike Black Dice, his counterpart.

Black Dice was quiet the whole ride. He reminded me of a silent assassin. He was dark as midnight, with shoulder length long hair. His hair was styled in micro French braids, but they appeared to be turning into dreads. I was tempted to ask if he wanted me to re-braid them for him, but I was afraid. He was a big black swole dude, and stood about six foot two. Also, he was so quiet I didn't know how to read him. Even when I hopped in the truck and said "Hi," he only nodded and said, "Wassup".

As we rolled to Hawthorne, Charlie said, "Look, ma, I'ma give you and Mo'nique y'all own apartments. You will work under me, and Mo'nique will work under my man, Maine. My sister is also one of my workers. My sister name is Chocolate. She's moving into her apartment today too, so y'all can get to know each other while getting' y'all houses together."

I couldn't believe my ears. Charlie was a super balla. He had apartments in Hawthorne and was just handing them out. I wanted to ask what he meant by me being his worker. I'd heard stories on how pimps picked up girls in my situation, treated them good, then pimped them out. However, I stayed quiet, and Charlie kept talking.

"Since I know yo' real age," he said, "I will not have you doing anythin' out of the ordinary. Your house will be my safe house. I will take you shoppin', plush it out, and have Chocolate teach you how to drive. My other sister, Joyce, will be staying with Chocolate. She's eighteen, so I will be buyin' all three of y'all cars. Peewee and Black Dice are my lead lieutenants, so if one of them tells you to do something, do it. They'll never tell you something that's not good for your sake..."

At that moment, Peewee yelled, "Daphne, get down!"

My heart skipped a beat. I almost jumped out of my seat and pissed on myself. I was so scared, the words 'get down' didn't register in my head. I just turned around and looked at Peewee like 'nigga why you just do that stupid shit?'

Charlie started laughing. "Ma, I just told you whateva my two lieutenants tell you to do, you do! See, if somebody was attackin' us, you woulda been dead or seriously hurt because you didn't listen."

"I understand. But Peewee, you didn't have to scare me like dat."

"Look girl," Peewee countered, "Charlie runs dis whole operation, but I run dis operation on the West Coast. When I tell yo' thick ass to do something, do it! Even if I tell yo' young thick ass to bend over, do it!"

I looked at Charlie and he didn't say nothing to Peewee about his statement, so I took it upon myself to check Peewee.

"Peewee, I understand whachu talking about, but I'm not bending over for no one. I'm still a virgin, and nigga you not my type."

When I said, virgin, Charlie's eyes lit up. Peewee, on the other hand, got frustrated. He said, "Cuzz, I'm not talkin' bout nothin' like dat. It was just a figure of speech. But like I said, if I say bend over, just bend over. And if I stick my dick in yo' pussy, it's only for yo' own good. Remember dat!"

When we arrived at the apartments in Hawthorne, Mo'nique hopped out of Maine's Benz all smiles. I knew he must have told her something good. She couldn't even grab her clothes out of the car without smiling. I wanted to ask her why she was so happy, but Charlie grabbed me by the arms and told me to follow his lead. He then told Peewee and Black Dice to meet him in the last apartment, and we walked off. Mo'nique and Maine were right behind us.

Charlie's apartment was nice. It had a security gate, so he had to let us in with keys since no one was home to buzz us in. Once we were in the complex, I was impressed with the unique design. Apartments #1 and #2 sat on top of each other. Then down the walkway were apartments #3 and #4. This structure was made to fit ten apartments all down one row. The last apartment was unit #10, and it was the apartment Peewee, Black Dice, Bull, and Bunch went into.

Charlie took me to apartment #3 and Maine and Mo'nique walked up the side stairs to apartment #4. For some reason, they wanted us to be in the front, but I was wondering why they didn't let us get the first two apartments.

"Why I can't get the first apartment?" I asked.

"Ma, you makin' dis hard on me. It's best to just listen and follow my lead. Don't ask too many questions, because I'ma start thinkin' you the Feds or something. Plus, Ma, I do er' thin' for a reason."

Charlie was only seventeen, so I wondered how in the hell did he orchestrate all his moves so well? He was smart, but I still wanted to know why I couldn't get the first apartment. I wanted to be able to look out my window and see the streets.

"Charlie, I'm not tryna make nothing hard on you, but I was just asking because I wanted the first apartment."

Charlie snapped. "Look! Shawty, if you don't wanna be here, I could take you right back where I got you. I'm doing you a favor, and I might be the best thing that could ever happen to you."

I had run my mouth a little too much and a little too soon.

Charlie fumed, "Ma, I'm not your father. Either you gon' follow my lead or we can shut dis down before it even start. In all honesty, I don't even mess with females my age or younger, so you should be happy. Now, if you just be quiet and let me show you around your house, you'll know why I don't want you in the front apartment."

I nodded and stayed quiet. Guilt consumed me, and tears moistened my eyes. I tried to hide them, but Charlie noticed.

"Whachu cryin' fo'?"

"Because I really like you," I replied. "And I'm messing up. I lied to you yesterday, and I'm gettin' on your nerves today. I have never been around a boy who really likes me enough to give me my own apartment."

Charlie was smooth. He grabbed my hand and gave me a kiss. I backpedaled and said, "I'm not too good at kissin', so don't be mad at me."

He grabbed my cheeks with both hands and stuck his tongue down my throat. I felt moist between the legs.

"Yeah, ma, don't worry. I'm an amateur at kissin' also. Not too many females get these. So, dry those eyes. Stop cryin'. Anyone in their right mind would inquire about their next move in life. That's why I just chuckled when Peewee said what he said. See, we are all family here. Peewee will never try to fuck you without my permission. Loyalty and respect is a big factor here. If I tell my boys you are my girl and to watch over you, that's what they gon' do. Even if that means catching a bullet for you; that's what they gone do. So what Peewee was tellin' you a minute ago is for yo' own good.

"Now, I didn't let you move into the first apartment for yo' own sake. For some odd reason, niggaz in Cali be hatin'. They hate for a nigga like me to come out here and set up shop in their hood. They hate that I can pull ten to twenty million outta their hood, when they can't pull a dime. These Cali niggaz are unorganized and kill each other over a muhfuckin' color."

"Shawty, to make a long story short, I'm against you being in that front apartment because if some nigga decides to ride on me and shoot up my apartment, I don't want you to be on the front line. Plus, apartments #1 and #2 are being used."

As Charlie talked, I paid close attention. He was talking with passion as if he really cared about my well-being. As he talked and showed me my two-bedroom apartment, his cell phone went off. At the same time, Maine and Mo'nique knocked on the door.

He said, "Hol' on," and answered his phone.

This would become the story of my life. Moments interrupted and me listening to Charlie's end of a phone call.

"Yo."

"Yeah, I'm down here in apartment #3."

"Come on. Yeah, we bout ta go shoppin'."

"Naw! All that other stuff at yo' old house, let it stay there. I'ma give that spot to Peewee for one of our workers.

"Chocolate, as long as you got all yo' important shit outta that crib, don't worry about that shit. What I tell you last night?"

"Yeah, that's exactly what I said, so let me handle dis. A'ight?"

"A'ight. We'll talk as soon as you get down here. And tonight is a no go on that other thing. I got my shawty down here, so come meet her."

"Okay."

"One."

I listened to Charlie talk to his sister, and I knew they had a unique bond. I became nervous because I didn't know what Charlie's sister was going to think of me. My hope was that she'd accept me with open arms.

When Charlie hung up, he said, "Go let yo' homegirl and Maine in."

He handed me a set of keys and said, "Don't lose 'em. Get an extra set made and hide them somewhere that only me and you can find 'em. Also, dis unit hold special value to me, so take special care of it. Anywayz, do you know how to cook?

I nodded. "Yep."

"What?"

"Everything!" I replied.

"Okay. We'll see."

"Yo, B, open the door!" Maine shouted.

We had forgotten about Maine and Mo'nique until Maine started banging on the door again and yelling. I ran to answer the door, but before I could answer it, Charlie grabbed my arm and swung me back to him.

He stuck his tongue down my throat again, and said, "Tonight, after we plush this house out, we're sleeping in the same bed, you dig?"

"What a straight to the point-ass nigga you are," I said. "You sho' don't wait, huh?"

"Shit, why wait when one day we might be walking down the aisle together. In all honesty, I've always told myself if I find a woman who I de-virginize and mold her as a thugette and my queen, I'll marry her and slow down. And I believe you have the potential to be my queen, so tonight it's going down."

Later that night around ten-thirty, after I'd come back from the mall with Chocolate, her son Michael, Joyce, Mo'nique, and Charlie, I found myself sitting on my new $6500 Italian leather sofa gossiping with Mo'nique. We talked about how when we met Chocolate, she looked at me up and down with a twisted face before saying, "Hi." I took it as she was just sizing me up. I guess she was trying to see if I was good enough for her brother, because after meeting her, she became cool. Joyce was cool with me right off the bat. She was Chocolate's younger sister, yet she had Chocolate by two inches. Chocolate was five foot nine, and Joyce was five foot eleven.

As we gossiped, I thought about Charlie. He was turning out to be more than just a nigga I'd just met a day before. I mean, he treated me ten times better in one day than my father had my whole life. I looked around my house and everything was plushed out. When we got back from the mall, I had a brand new stove, refrigerator, dining table, china cabinet, and all the house necessities. My leather couches and 62-inch big screen television were moved in by Peewee and Black Dice. In my room, I had a king size bed that sat 42-inches off the ground, so I had to climb up the side to get in it. My house was plushed with stainless steel appliances. I even had jet black silk curtains that Charlie had personally put up for me.

Charlie closed off the second bedroom in my house, and told me, "Don't go in there until I tell you." He put a Master lock on the door, and I knew not to question him, because he did everything for a reason. I thought that maybe he had something in there to surprise me with later on.

As I thought of Charlie, my new cell phone, that he bought m, went off. The only people who had my number were Charlie, his crew, Mo'nique, Chocolate, and Joyce, so I wasn't surprised when I answered and Charlie said, "Yo."

"Thinking of the devil." I shot into the phone.

"Ooh, I'm the devil now, huh, ma? Shit, I coulda sworn after somebody spends over $60,000 on you in one day, that person is like an angel of God. See, on the West y'all so ungrateful, you still haven't said, 'baby thank you for the house, bed, couch, phone, TV, or nothing.' I mean, you see at the mall you got two times more than my sisters and yo' homegirl. So you shouldn't be thinkin' of no devil, but a god."

I chuckled. Charlie was right. I didn't thank him like I was supposed to. I felt bad, and said, "I'm sorry for not showing my appreciation, but since you said you want that tonight, I'll try to show my appreciation then."

"That sounds good. But right now, I'm back here in apartment #10 with Maine and the rest of my crew handling some bidness, so I won't be home until twelve. Order some pizza or something for you and Mo'nique if y'all get hungry, but if not, you best go get ready for big daddy."

I laughed, "Is that right?"

"Ma, I'm as serious as a heart attack. So tell Mo'nique to go home. Maine will be up there to attend to her, and you go wash that ass."

"Charlie, if that's what you want, you can get it. Your wish is my command."

"Ma, that's what's up. So we'll holla as soon as I get down there. I gotta go."

"One."

When I hung up, Mo'nique started laughing. She said, "Damn, you didn't tell me you were going to give it up already. I guess Mr. Charlie is a smooth operator."

I shook my head and replied, "Life goes on."

Around midnight, I was just hopping out of the tub and Mo'nique was long gone. I wasn't hungry, so I didn't order any pizza. I was still full from all the food I ate at the mall.

Charlie walked through the door as I stood in the bathroom drying off. I had my right leg arched on the tub and the bathroom door was wide open. From the front door, you could see straight into the bathroom, so he said, "I musta came home at the right time."

I was surprised and nervous. I didn't know what to do. My instinct told me to cover up, but I had already promised him that I was all his.

I kept drying off, and he said, "Ma, you are beautiful. You are beautiful from head to toe. I love them thick thighs and them pretty brown eyes. You make a young nigga wanna eat you…"

Charlie was talking nice and smooth. I can't lie, just by him talking to me and complimenting my well-sculpted body, I was turned on. I could feel the heat between my thighs, and knew it was about time for me to lose my virginity.

Charlie walked over to me and cupped my womanhood. I was still nervous, but I let him do what he had to do. He looked in my eyes as he massaged my clitoris. My love button stiffened and my juices leaked onto his fingers.

He kissed me on the ear and whispered, "Ma, don't worry. I got you."

As he caressed me, a low moan escaped. His fingers felt like magic. When he felt I was wet enough, he stuck his middle finger inside me. I gasped for air, but everything he was doing felt good. There was a little pain, but the pleasure outweighed everything; even my thoughts of protection.

Charlie started fingering my womb while my right leg was still arched on the tub. He went to work and my eyes crawled to the back of my head. I moaned nonstop until I had my first orgasm. It felt like I had to pee, but I knew what it was from the intense pleasure that almost buckled my knees.

When I shouted, "Oh my Gawd!" Charlie knew what time it was. He took his finger out of me and started kissing and sucking on my neck. I never even knew that my neck was directly connected to my pussy. Between my legs, I was wetter than Niagara Falls.

After Charlie sucked on my neck for about five minutes, he moved down to my breasts. He whispered, "Ma, I love the size of these perky things. I can bet my last dime these are some 36Cs."

I was convinced that Charlie was a sex genius. He knew my breast size right off top. He nibbled on my nipples, and it was as if he just demanded for me to nut. The sensation he caused was unbelievable. I didn't know I could have an orgasm from someone just sucking and nibbling on my breasts, until he made me explode for the second time.

My whole body shivered as I came, and Charlie whispered, "That's what I'm talking about. Cum for me, ma." He held my left nipple with his right index finger and thumb while he licked my belly button. His tongue then parted my lower lips and invaded my body. I moved his fingers from my nipples and started massaging them myself, my excitement grew as I pleasured my own body.

Charlie said, "Ma, I guess, you ready to go in the room."

The whole time in the bathroom, Charlie never undressed. He attended to me and took me places I'd never been. After he carried me to our room like Hercules, he stripped out of his clothes.

I looked at his manhood and said, "Whoa!" He measured about nine-inches, and I wondered what I was supposed to do with that.

Charlie must've read my thoughts. "Look, ma, I'm going to take it nice and slow. I'ma let you control the speed. Then, after you catch on, we're gonna get a little freaky. I wanna taste you, and want you to taste me. Sex and love is a beautiful thang, so let's go all out," he said.

After Charlie made his statement, I lay in bed with my legs spread eagle. Charlie climbed on top of me, but didn't stick his penis directly in me. He used it to play with my clitoris. He was teasing me and all hell broke loose. My floodgates broke. I was cumming nonstop. I oohed and aahed as he teased me. I was on fire.

Even though I didn't know too much about sex, I was ready to lose my virginity. The pleasure I was receiving without any penetration felt so good, I wanted to feel the real thing. I took hold of his penis and slowly slid it inside me. The head of his dick split me open about five centimeters, expanding my treasure box to receive him. The pain was so overwhelming. I tried to take it like a real woman, but I still told him to be gentle.

He started off slowly. I felt every inch of his penis dig into me. When he picked up the pace, I moaned and cried.

"Oh my gawd!"

"Oh my gawd!"

"Charlie, I love it!"

"I love it!"

"Oh my gawd!"

"This feels soo good!"

"Oh my gawd!"

"Stop, please stop!"

"Oh my gawd!"

"No, don't stop!"

"Oh my gawd!"

"I love you!"

"Oooooooooh!"

"Charlie, a little faster!"

Charlie took me to La-La Land and beyond. He pounded harder and harder. I nutted about five times before he released his fluids inside of me and collapsed right on top of me with his penis still nestled in my cookie. I felt his warm semen enter my vaginal canal, but thought nothing of it. My pussy was throbbing from its first beat down, and Charlie was ready to go some more rounds. He hopped off me, pulled his penis out of me, and buried his face between my legs.

I loved every bit of his head game. My heart started beating a hundred miles per hour. He was teasing my clitoris with the tip of his tongue like he teased it with his penis. I gripped the sheets, low moans turned into loud screams. My pussy filled back up with cum. I was on top of the world in fantasyland. I didn't know what he was doing to me, but my first sexual experience was turning out great.

By the time Charlie removed his face from between my legs, the bed had a puddle of my fluids. He looked at me and I was sweating like a felon on a high-speed chase. My body was dripping wet. We'd been going at it for four hours.

He teased, "You like that?"

I blushed. "You know I do."

"Well, it's yo' turn."

I didn't want to suck Charlie's dick, but his penis was now a part of me. After all he had taken me through, I felt I had to reward him. I thought about all the times I sucked on popsicles, and went to work. For my first time giving a blowjob, I did it to the extreme. Charlie came within no time once I started slurping and sucking his dick.

As he approached his peak, he said, "You did better than I thought. Now swallow, don't spit! It's a privilege to have me cum in yo' mouth and down yo' throat."

I felt violated. I did not want to swallow his sperm, but why spoil the moment?

I swallowed.

The next morning, Charlie was up watching the Family network on cable when I woke up. They were airing a show about black folks. Two black college students from Clark University hosted the show. They touched on topics that affected the black community, such as prisons, higher learning, low income, jealousy, hate, destruction, baby momma drama, fatherless homes, and so on.

As the brother on the show talked about a baby momma conflict one of his boys was going through, I fell into deep thought. I'd actually given myself to a complete stranger. I didn't know too much about Charlie, but he knew everything about me. I didn't know his last name, his mother's name, his background, or nothing. Did he have any kids? Where specifically on the East Coast was he from? I knew he told me Queens, but he also told me he stayed all over New York. I didn't know what type of business he actually indulged in. I didn't know what he actually had in store for me. I interrupted the show and spoke my mind.

Charlie smiled. "Ma, I see this show is getting to you, so let me help your inquiring mind. I was born and raised in Queens, New York. Started thuggin' at age eleven when my mother, Mrs. Mary K. Warner started struggling to pay rent because of a drug habit. My last name is Warner. And right now, that's all you need to know. I told you about asking so many questions. Only the Feds do that."

Charlie had warned me about questioning him, but I needed to know if he had any kids. I mean, we didn't use any protection, so I knew there was a chance of me getting pregnant. I felt stupid for giving myself to a complete stranger.

"Charlie, I don't know how you feel about me, but I need to know more about you. I mean, you did fuck me without a condom. I honestly don't know nothing about you, and I feel like a hoe."

"Naw, ma, don't feel that way. I know we started off fast, but believe me, everything happens for a reason."

"So why is it hard for you to tell me more about yourself?"

"Well, if me tellin' you more about myself will get you in that kitchen, let me start. Because as my woman, you gotta know how to cook for my whole crew."

"As your woman, I believe I'm supposed to do that anyway, so can you please answer all my questions?"

"Look, ma, I don't normally get down like this, but you're my new and only shawty, so check it out. I'm a hustla. I move shit from coast to coast. I have a team in mostly every state. But since I mess with the Mexicans across the border, I've settled in Cali. I let you move in this apartment because it was love at first sight and I need a secretary. There's nothing better than having a Bonnie. I learned the game from my older brother. His name was JR. He got killed out here in Cali. He was at the wrong place, at the wrong time. The Bloods and Crips were having a shootout and he just so happened to be driving by. A bullet ripped through his Lexus and hit him in the neck..."

As Charlie talked, tears filled his eyes. I knew the loss of his brother was a major loss to him. I felt it was my job to give him a hug and let him know it was all right.

I hugged him and kissed him on the forehead. "Baby, it's all right, you can talk to me about anything."

I knew Charlie had his feelings built up inside him and needed someone to talk to, so I let him vent.

"My brother raised me. My mother was a crackhead. I had no father. He gave up on life and gave it to Coke and Rum, Bacardi and Gin, and anything that could take him to another world. Due to the struggle, my brother had to give up his football scholarship after three years of college. Since he was enrolled at USC before he had to come back to Queens to take care of me, he had met a lot of Los Angeles street playas, thugs, and gangstas.

"Before my brother received word that our parents were all the way gone and I was living on the streets, I had formed a little crew and we were out getting money any way possible. Since Maine and I were boys since birth and we both had parents who didn't care, we hustled together. We were full-fledged street thugs by the time my brother came back to Queens. We were only eleven, but we knew the jungle creed must feed.

"JR introduced us to hustling. His roommate in college was this fat Mexican named Jorge. Jorge had a big family that was connected to the Mexican mafia. My brother ended up marrying and having two daughters by Jorge's sister, Jessica, so when he decided to become a full time hustla, we already had big connections. Using his college connections, my brother formed a team outta my crew, his boys he grew up with, and the crew he hung with in college. He started in Queens, then moved to Harlem, Manhattan, New Jersey, Atlanta, Washington

D.C. and a few other states and cities before finally moving to Cali with my sister-in-law and their kids."

"To make a long story short, my brother had a team and empire worth over ten million annually before he died, so when he died, I inherited everything. I already knew the game, so now I have you and my own squad."

Charlie's story was deep. I found myself in tears. We cuddled like we'd known each other for years. I wanted to ask more about him and his family, but I thought better of it. I wondered where Chocolate was during all their trials, because he never mentioned her or Joyce.

I decided not to ask more questions about his family, because I had stirred up lots of emotions within him already. However, I needed to know if he had any kids. I knew he had a lot of sex expertise. I assumed with his knowledge of how to touch and manipulate a woman's body, he had at least two baby mommas.

I said, "Charlie, you still haven't answered my initial question. Do you have any kids? At least let me know so I can prepare. I mean, you see the host talking about how baby mommas bring so much drama."

He ignored my question for about five minutes before saying, "Not to my knowledge."

His answer didn't sit too well with me. I started thinking of another approach, but his cell phone went off.

It was Maine. He was upstairs with Mo'nique, but he was telling Charlie to meet him in the back.

Charlie hopped up and said, "I gotta go. Here's five thousand. Spend it how you want."

Chapter 4

Charlie

Julie and Juliet, my nieces, were getting big. I'd been at my sister-in-law's house for an hour and some change playing with my brother's daughters and talking to Jessica. The last time I'd seen my brother's family was at his funeral; that had been a little over a year ago, and so much had changed. I was traveling from state to state, coast to coast, and running the streets like a chicken with my head cut off. All in all, I was doing so much, I was running from reality.

Reality was, I had priorities and kids that I was neglecting, and some I wasn't even accepting. I was neglecting all of my children. I was neglecting my mother, who was a year clean and free of drugs. And was neglecting my brother's wife and the two angels he'd left behind.

I was caught up in the street life. I had a team of hustlers, killers, and go-getters that all needed my attention and leadership. I had eight women who I couldn't shake or get off my mind. I was only in love with one, but couldn't open up and tell her my deepest secrets. I was a leader, but my weakness was pussy. I was addicted to sex, and I needed help.

Jessica was the closest thing I had to my brother. She was his backbone and helped him raise me. She was twenty-six and the thickest Latina I'd ever known. She was also the smartest woman I'd ever met. At times, I wondered if my brother had anything to do with the way she carried herself, or if she was this way before they. met. I mean, if I didn't know any better, I would have sworn she had some black in her. Where does my brother come into play? I don't know, but Jessica was a strong, smart, and loyal woman. She had all the traits of a black woman.

She sensed something was wrong with me and said, "Choo-Choo." She nicknamed me Choo-Choo two months after I came to Cali. She said I moved around from state to state like a train. That was in my early days of hustling when I was what we called a runner. That's when Maine and I was doing drop-offs for my brother.

"Choo-Choo, keep it real! What's wrong? I know you didn't come out here to only see yo' nieces, so what's wrong? Because you talk to em' er' day. Plus, you got Peewee and Dice just waiting outside. They been out there for the last two hours, so what you wanna talk about? What, Jorge ain't called you or something?"

Jorge was my supplier, and Jessica's brother. He was also my brother's best friend. I talked to him daily, so he wasn't a problem. He was actually like an older brother to me. I know if I had a problem with him, I could have gone to him.

"Jess, Jorge don't got nothing to do with this. This has to do with me and all the cards life has dealt me."

Jessica frowned. "Choo, what did you do this time?" She was used to me messing up and coming to her for support. Like one time, I wrecked my brother's Porsche. I told her first. I asked her, "How do I tell JR I wrecked his car while showing off on Crenshaw?" She told me to just tell him it was an accident, and that I'll pay for it.

Her answer ended up working and my brother didn't trip.

I replied, "Jess, the question is what didn't I do?"

"Choo, just tell me. You been taking care of business like you supposed to? And I'm not talking about the streets either. I'm talking about them kids, because we have already been down this road."

"Jess, I got caught up in the streets again. It's like I'm stuck in the middle of a spider web. And it's killing me, because I know JR is turning over in his grave. He always told me to never be a deadbeat like our father. I send thousands to my kids er' month, but I need to be there physically for them, and I can't."

I felt tears rush to my eyes. My emotions started to rage. I was a failure as a man. I had just turned eighteen, and I had conceived my first child at fourteen. I had five in total, and four on the way.

Jessica shouted, "Choo, why can't you? All you gotta do is make visitin' arrangements. I can get Maria to let the twins come stay with me for a few weeks. If you woulda kept to the agreement last time, you'd probably have more of a bond with Little Charlie and Charlisa."

I felt guilty hearing Jessica go off. She was speaking the truth and it hurt. My ego was crushed. I was worth $50 million on the streets, but couldn't even take care of my kids. I had problems money couldn't fix. They say a man don't cry, but that's a lie. I cried often, thinking over my situation, and the fact that I was a deadbeat father.

I broke down in front of my nieces and they both ran into my arms. Julie was only six-years-old. She said, "Uncle Choo, don't cry." She wiped my tears with her thumb and gave me a hug.

Juliet, a year younger than Julie, added, "We love you."

Jessica was fuming at me. She loved me with all her heart, but she hated that I was living up to the statistics. The statistics were that 85% of Hispanic and African American males who conceived a baby before the age of eighteen will abandon that child due to immaturity. I was doing just that, and Jessica hated it. She told my nieces not to console me, and sent them to their rooms.

When they were out of the living room, Jessica blurted, "Charlie!"

When she called me Charlie, she was serious.

"Charlie, I don't know what's wrong with you. Are you smokin' your own supplies? You got flesh and blood out here that love you, but you love the streets more! And since you're doing the opposite of what your brother would be doing, I'ma give you an ultimatum. But before I do, I wanna know everything. And I know, somebody else is pregnant, because I've been eating a lot of chocolate lately, and I haven't had anybody in my life since your brother died."

Jessica knew me better than I knew myself. I knew I had lots of explaining to do, so I got right to it.

"Jess, I know you know about the twins and that situation. I didn't go through with our last agreement with Maria because the girl wanna kill me. She knows I had something to do with Rico and Carlos gettin' killed. I'm not stupid! I'm not bout to go out there for dat girl to set me up—"

I was immediately cut off. "Charlie, don't start making excuses. We both know that Maria loves you too much to kill you. Yes, she knows you had Peewee and Black Dice kill her brothers, but she ain't trippin'. She said she knew y'all were at war and somebody was going to die, so she stayed out of it'."

"Yeah right!" I blurted. "I know you don't believe that bullshit. Shit, we went to war over her stupid ass."

"Choo, don'tchu think I know that? She told me she told her brothers to stay out y'all mess, but they got into it and she couldn't stop 'em from trying to get you—"

"Bullshit!" I cut Jessica off. I had talked enough about Maria. I knew the problem with me and her was never going to change. I was 100% sure the twins were mine. All Jessica had to do was arrange with Maria for the kids to come to Cali. I had other baby momma problems to deal with. Maria was the least of my worries.

"Well, if you can get Maria to agree to let me keep the twins for the summer, I'll pay whatever it cost. However, right now, I wanna talk to you about my three maybes and the four on the way..."

"Four on the way!" Jessica repeated wide-eyed. "What do you mean, four on the way?"

Jessica was so angry she jumped up and started pacing the living room floor. She was my big sister/mother. Four more kids on the way to her meant I'd never taken her advice about using protection.

She snapped. "Charlie, you ain't going to learn until you catch something and your dick fall off! I wanna know about these four on the way, but finish telling me about the three maybes first."

"My three maybes are all in different states. You already know Shondella. She's from Cali. Tracy is a female from Philly. I never told you about her. She's twenty and claims her son is mine. Charlene just had our daughter. She's from Atlanta. "Jess, outta all three females, I believe, Charlene's daughter might be mine. The baby is only two-months-old, so I really don't know yet. Charlene was a good girl, but I was being a hoe like always, and she caught me cheatin'. For the whole year I stayed in the derty, she was down with me. She was my girl, no doubt. I never used a condom fuckin' her, so I believe Charlena might be mine. My only doubt is that she waited 'til I came back out here to Cali to tell me she was pregnant. Also, child-support was the first thing outta her mouth."

Jessica stopped pacing and sat on the end of her couch. Her left hand covered her face. She was shaking her head, indicating she wasn't too pleased with me. However, she stayed quiet.

I continued. "In Philly, Maine and I messed with Tracy. She was just a fuck thang to us. I think she's puttin' her two-year-old son, Tre, on me, because she knows I got money."

My sister in-law just shook her head. "Choo, you should just listen to yourself. You know how females get down, and you still put yourself in harm's way. How stupid is that?"

"Jess, what's done is done."

"So why in the hell are you still givin' every female you think is fuckable a chance to get you caught up? I swear I'm glad you didn't get yo' hoe' tendencies from JR."

"Shit, JR didn't have to start living in the streets at a young age. If he did, it'd be a different story. Yo, we ain't talking about my brother anywayz. We're talking about me."

"I know who we're talking about. Now get to Shondella's drama queen ass. It doesn't surprise me that you're denying her son, but let me hear your reason."

"Well, you already know how my brother felt about her. He said she ran her mouth too much, and not to mess with her. Shit, she was my first Cali girl and way ahead of my league. She had me sprung. Remember, I was only fifteen when I started messing with her. She was already eighteen with a track record that I knew nothing about. So, when she had Paul, I signed the birth certificate. I really thought he was mine, at first. But after having a few of my boys investigate, I've come to find out she is foul. She's a loud, triflin bitch. A straight up hoodrat."

Jessica said, "Whoa! I knew she was drama. But damn, not a hoodrat."

"Yeah, ma, that's the deal on shawty. What chu think I should do?"

"You're gonna bring me some money tomorrow, and I'ma go have some DNA tests taken. Anyhow, gone head and finish telling me about your baby momma drama, because now I wanna hear about the four on the way."

"Alright, check it out! I found the love of my life three and a half months ago. Her name is Daphne, and she's younger than me. She's fifteen, but when we met, she was fourteen and still a virgin. I got her kicked out her father's house, so I let her move in one of my apartment units. It's a long story, but Maine moved her best friend in an apartment unit too. They occupy units #3 and #4 in our complex. Her best friend's name is Mo'nique. She's from outta Watts, so you know there's some drama with her. However, the story is deeper than that. The same day Daphne and Mo'nique moved in, I moved in a stripper I'd met the night before. She's in apartment #9. Her name is Janet, but I call her Chocolate. She's originally from Washington D.C., but moved out here with her eighteen-year-old sister, Joyce, and four-year-old son..."

"Charlie, please don't tell me you fucked all four of these girls. If so, you're foul."

I shook my head. "I already know!"

"It's just that I couldn't control the temptation. I mean, I was only supposed to use Chocolate and her sister as my outta state drop off girls, but my small head outsmarted my big head."

"Do any of these girls know about each other? I mean, it's crazy for you to have all these girls pregnant and they are that close to each other."

"Well, it goes like this... Chocolate, Joyce, and Mo'nique all know that Daphne is my girl. They know

I love her. The twist is, I told Daphne that Chocolate and Joyce are my sisters. She don't know nothing. I feel bad because I know deep down in my heart this is the girl I wanna marry. I mean, I taught her everything and she's performing perfectly. The only thing is, she asked me about kids when we first got together, and I told her I don't have any. Now, she's three months pregnant. She's not for sure if she's pregnant or not, but I am."

"Choo, if you love this girl like you say, why are you doing her so bad? Shit, honestly, I know you love her because I've never heard you speak so highly about a woman."

"Jess, I swear, I don't be trying to do Daphne wrong! It's like the temptation won't leave. Take Mo'nique for example. A month after Maine moved Mo'nique in an apartment and taught her the same as his secretary he turned her out. I thought he was going to turn her into his West Coast girl, but you know he's still in love with Nikki in Miami. To make a long story short, I just so happened to be checking out our business unit early one morning when Maine and the rest of the crew were runnin' a train on her. I'd always wanted to fuck Mo'nique, so when Maine told me he don't care nothing about her, I jumped in line. After that day, I've been creeping with her on and off. I be in apartment #4 twice a week now."

"Damn, that's foul," Jessica blurted. "Choo, what if a female do you like that? You'll wanna kill her, right?"

My sister hit it right on the nose. I wouldn't have known how to handle it. I knew I would've done something stupid. I felt bad. I was doing Daphne wrong.

"Jess, you right. But what's done is done. That's why I'm here talking to you."

"Well, finish tellin' me the rest of the story, because yo' boys or should I say your bodyguards are still waiting on you. Tell me about Chocolate and her sister. How did you start sleeping with both of them? And how many months are they? Also, you forgot to tell me how many months Mo'nique is. By the way you just explained y'all situation, her baby might not be yours."

I shook my head in agreement.

"Mo'nique supposed to be two months pregnant. She told me the baby might be mine, but anybody in my crew could be the father. To keep Daphne from finding out, she saying the baby is Maine's."

"Choo, this shit is crazy! You're only eighteen! You got too much baby momma drama. You need to be more cautious about AIDS, because seems to me, you love living up to that bullshit nickname of yours, B.B. King!"

"Jess, it's not like that. I just hate condoms. I even think I'm allergic to 'em. Also, er' time I use one, it break..."

"BULLSHIT! Choo, your dick is not that big! You can sell that to some other Mexican girl who don't speak English, but nigga not me. You must forgot I put up with your brother for almost a decade before he passed."

"Anyways! Let's get back to the other two on the way."

"You sho' know how to take charge, don'tchu?"

Jessica cracked a small smile. "That's what I'm supposed to do. I can't just sit back and let chu crash into a brick wall. Your brother will hop out his grave and kill me."

"I bet he will."

"But anyway, I had sex with Chocolate the same night I met her. The condom broke and I kept going. I had planned not to fuck her no more after I got with

Daphne, but she was too much of a freak for me not to. I've been fucking her like two to three times a week. She says she's three months pregnant, but I doubt that the baby is mine because she was sellin' pussy before I met her. Now, Joyce was the last one I stuck my dick into. I ended up fuckin' her because I had just sent her and Chocolate to Boston to drop some work off and pick up some money. When they got back to L.A., I told Chocolate to take the money to Daphne. Daphne babysits Chocolate's son when she goes outta town. Daphne also controls all the money and makes sure each member of my team is taken care of. You already know about the three safes in her apartment, so I don't gotta explain too much. But when I told Chocolate to take that money to Daphne, I told Joyce to ride with me to go pick up something to eat."

"As we drove to Red Dragon's, I felt like testin' my luck. I wondered if she was a freak like her sister. I asked was she a freak, and she asked why. I said, 'because I wanna know.' To make a long story short, I fucked her in the back of my truck. Now, she's supposed to be pregnant. I've fucked Joyce a few times now, so her baby might be mine."

"Choo, I'm glad you came and told me all this, because nine children by eight different women is outrageous. I want you to go with me to get an AIDS test. I'm sorry to say, but if you don't, I don't want you around your nieces until you do. I know I'm putting up a harsh ultimatum, but it's only for your own good. I need you to bring me about fifty thousand tomorrow, so I can go to the courts with my attorney and file for paternity tests. I need the numbers to all your baby mommas. I wanna get their info, because we 'bout to find out who's not. Drama queens like Shondella aren't gonna take a test, but my lawyer will have a judge order her. Choo, with all these kids, you gotta give the street life up. I want you to put up about two million, and I'll invest it in my food chains. I also wanna open a grocery store. This was your brother's dream, so I'ma live it out through you. However, I'm going to need some time to get my operation started, so please keep your dick protected and your team tight."

I left Jessica's house feeling a little relieved. I had put myself in a stressful situation, and it was killing me. I was warned by many people to stop playing with fire, but I never listened. They say a hard head makes a soft ass, and I was learning the hard way.

As soon as I hopped in my truck, Peewee said, "Cuzz, don't say nothing! Keep yo' head straight and drive!"

I sensed the urgency in his voice and did as told. When I got away from my folk's house, I asked, "Yo, what's the deal?"

Whenever Peewee talked in a stone voice, I knew he was serious and something was happening out of the ordinary. I heard Black Dice in the back seat assembling one of his machine guns, and thought, *damn! My own niggas bout to take me down.*

I kept my eyes on the road, but thought of all the possibilities that could have gone down. My two lieutenants didn't tell me what was going on until we got to the 101 freeway.

Peewee said, "Look! While you were in Jessica's house, we noticed that black Baretta behind us has been followin' us. We don't know who it is. We don't know if it's the Feds or if it's some young niggas tryna put in some work on us. So, don't get on the freeway. Drive down this one way to the dead end. Speed up so you can bust a U turn. Dice and I gone hop out before you hit the turn, so just sit tight."

I accelerated the car and grabbed my 9 from my waist. I looked in my rearview and the black Barretta was right on my bumper. It had tinted windows, so I couldn't see inside. I knew it was more than three people in the car, but I couldn't recognize anyone.

Damn! Why do these Cali niggaz be trippin'?

When I got to the dead end, Peewee yelled, "Stop!"

He and Black Dice leapt out of my truck so fast, I didn't get a chance to stop all the way. The next thing I heard was, "Aww bitch! Are you crazy?"

I hit the U turn, turned my truck off and hopped out. It was Shondella, with my son and three of her homegirls.

Dice looked at me and said, "Man, I almost killed her." Dice never talked, so I knew I had to check Shondella.

"Yo, what tha fuck wrong witchu? Ma, I told you about doin' stupid ass shit!"

I wanted to just slap the shit out of Shondella. She stayed doing some dumb shit. I mean, she was known for slashing my tires, keying my cars, breaking my windows, and starting drama for no apparent reason.

I drew my hand back to slap the taste out of her mouth, but Peewee grabbed it. "Homie, don't even let this bitch get you outta character. She wants you to put your hands on her. We know the game, let's bounce."

Shondella frowned. "Peewee, who's talkin' to yo' crab ass?" She was playing with fire.

I told my boys to go wait in the truck. Shondella knew that calling Peewee a crab was offensive. He was a Crip, and calling a Crip a crab is like a white man calling a black man a nigga; it's very rude and disrespectful. Shondella lived for drama, but today I wasn't going to bite.

I sent my boys to the truck and asked Shondella, "What tha hell do you want?"

"Nigga, yo' son wanted to see you! And I need some money."

"Yo, I just sent you some money yesterday. What happened to that?"

"I spent it! Paul needed some clothes and stuff, and I rented this Baretta."

"So you just do anythin' you want with my money, huh?"

"Shit, it's mine once you give it to me. As long as Paul is taken care of, you shouldn't worry about what I do with the money. You should be glad I don't file for child support!"

I was fed up with Shondella. I was fed up with all the baby momma drama. I snapped.

"Bitch, do what you gotta do! You ain't getting shit else from me. From now on, I'll buy Paul clothes and shoes when I think he need some, and I'ma drop er' thing off at yo mom's house. And since you want child support, I want a paternity test, so you can get it outcha ass bitch if he ain't mine." I blew Shondella away with my statement.

"What? Now, you wanna test? I'm not takin' no goddamn test when you know Paul is yo goddamn son.

I looked at Shondella, flicked a dollar on the ground, and said, "I hope so," and walked off.

When I hopped back in my truck, Peewee said, "Man, you got issues!"

I shook my head and replied, "I know."

Chapter 5

Daphne

It happened so fast. I was pregnant! I'd only been messing with Charlie for four months and I was three months pregnant. I knew it was only a matter of time before I conceived, but everything just happened so fast. I mean, after our first sexual encounter, Charlie and I had been going at it ever since. I was surprised because every female in the apartments was pregnant.

Mo'nique was pregnant by Maine. Chocolate was pregnant by her son's father, and Joyce was pregnant by her boyfriend, whoever that was. With the three of them pregnant, I felt good about being pregnant. I wasn't alone.

I called my mother and told her the news. She said I was too young and should have an abortion. Charlie and I had already talked about the baby and we were keeping it. And, in all honesty, I was in love with him and knew with a baby I'd always have him.

I told my mother my plans, and she said, "Daphne, if Charlie really loves you, you don't gotta have a baby to keep him."

My mother was a complete hypocrite with her statement. Truth be told, she had me to keep my no good father around, and this was after she found out he had more than fifteen other kids by ten different women. I hissed, "See Momma, this is the same reason I didn't want to call you. You did the same thing with my father. The only difference between me and you is, Charlie don't have any kids. My father had damn near twenty."

My mother countered, "That's just what I'm talking about. Daphne, I don't want chu to be like me. Your father told me the same thing Charlie telling you. He swore you were going to be his only child, but you see what happened. Daphne, you should have an abortion and just come back home. Please!"

My mother was trying everything in her power to get me to come back home and to have an abortion, but it wasn't happening. I had it too good. I had my own two bedroom apartment, a brand new Lexus, and a wardrobe filled with DKNY, Fendi, Guess, Gucci, and Calvin Klein. At age fifteen, I thought I was on top of the world. I mean, tell me what fifteen-year-old girl you know had it like me?

I replied, "Momma, I told you, I am not coming back to that house. I'm free where I'm at. I'm okay, and I can live life. Besides, you know my father has always said, 'once you're out, stay out' I'm not going to give him the satisfaction of slamming the door in my face."

"Well, Daphne, since you wanna be stupid like I was when I was your age, don't come crying to me when things go wrong."

Click!

My mother hung up in my face. I became irate and slammed my phone onto the holder and hissed, "You stupid bitch!" My relationship with my mother was on and off, and my relationship with my father was non-existent. I felt stupid for calling her.

I paced around my living room, mad at myself for giving my mother the satisfaction of hanging up in my face, then my phone rang again. I thought, *Oh! This bitch wanna call back, huh?*

I answered. "What?"

A female blurted. "Damn, You sho' don't know how to answer a phone."

I snapped. "Who dis?"

"Bitch, don't worry about who dis. Just tell Charlie's no good ass, Paul needs some shoes and I need some money!"

Click!

I had been hung up on twice within one minute. I was hotter than fish grease. I didn't know what to do. I wanted to ask the heifer who she was, and who was Paul. I wanted to check her for calling me out of my name, and I wanted to ask her how she knew my man, and how did she get my number.

I picked up my phone and dialed *69, but the number was blocked. I hissed, "Damn!" and slammed the phone back down. I started thinking about my father. He had women calling my house at all times asking for stuff. I was hoping Paul wasn't Charlie's son. I was hoping Charlie didn't play me like my father did my mother.

I thought about every possibility while waiting for Charlie to come home. I thought so hard I got a headache. My stomach even started fluttering. The talk with my mother was the only thing in my head. I even heard her voice roaring in my head, *Girl, he's no good! He's just like your father.*

My head was spinning, so I stretched out on the couch. The next thing I know, I was sleep and some bald headed female with a little boy, who looked just like Charlie, popped in my dream.

The female was saying, "Yeah, bitch! This Charlie's son."

The little boy added, "Charlie is my daddy."

My eyes widened. "Damn, Charlie stuck his dick in you?"

"Yeah, bitch, and he ate my pussy and licked my ass. So if you kissed him, let's say you had some of my pussy and ass too."

I grabbed my gun Charlie left in the house for me, and that was all I remembered. I was awakened by a knock at my door. I thought, *oh shit! My nightmare is about to become a reality. The bitch is here!*

"Daphne, it's me! Open the door, girl," Chocolate yelled as she knocked.

I didn't want to open the door, I didn't want to be bothered. I was stressed over the two phone calls. I wanted to tell Chocolate I'm busy, but I didn't want her to think I was doing something her brother wouldn't approve of. Chocolate and I were becoming good friends. I babysat for her when she had to go out of state. Her son was my son two weeks out of each month. I felt she was family, but I was having a vibe that she was only putting up a front. I didn't know where this vibe was coming from, but my woman's intuition was telling me that Chocolate was crafty. I thought it was from the thought that her brother probably had her watching me, so I never really paid it any mind.

I let Chocolate in, and she said, "Girl, I was just comin' to see what were you doin'."

I wanted to say, "I'm waiting on your no good ass brother. His baby momma called my mutherfuckin' house." However, I replied, "Shit, I'm not doing too much. I'm bout to go upstairs and see if Mo'nique wanna roll to the projects to get her sister."

I was lying to get Chocolate out of my house, but she asked, "Can I roll?"

I ended up agreeing and we marched upstairs.

Mo'nique was on the phone when we made it in her house. She was talking to Maine and rolling her eyes as if he was saying something she didn't like. Maine, Bull, and Bunch stayed going out of state, so Mo'nique was their mule. She kept all their supplies. Maine would cook cocaine before he left, and Mo'nique would wait until they called with the address to ship the dope to them.

Out of all the women in the complex, I had the best job. All I had to do was babysit, collect money, put it in a safe, cook, clean the house, and make sure everybody in our crew was taken care of. Charlie had it that everything except his merchandise came through me. I had the best position a woman in the streets could ever ask for.

Quiet as it's kept, Charlie had it set where the two of us never touched his merchandise. If you didn't know, you would have thought Maine was the man with the master plan. You would have thought he was the one with all the money, but just like most outsiders, you would have been wrong.

I once asked Charlie why would he put his best friend in such a situation where it's a chance he could get caught up. Charlie replied, "Maine is hard headed. He don't wanna give the street life up. He like going from state to state posing as the big man. I've told him a thousand times to kick back, but he feels he gotta be involved in everything."

As Mo'nique talked to Maine, I looked at her and shook my head. She said, "Well, Maine, I sent you your last package already, so we'll talk later. Because I'm 100% sure, I know who nutted in me."

I thought, *uh-oh! Somebody is having baby daddy drama already.* I kind of knew about two weeks after we moved in that Maine didn't really like Mo'nique. It was something about the way he treated her that let me know it was more to it than meet the eyes. However, I said nothing about it. Mo'nique was acting as if she was in love, so I didn't want to break her heart.

When she hung up, I asked, "Mo'nique, have you talked to your sister?"

Mo'nique looked at me and replied, "Why?"

I wanted to say, "Bitch, don't be snappin' at me because you and yo baby daddy ain't getting along." However, I said, "Because me and Chocolate about to go get her."

"How y'all gonna do that when she's at a track meet right now?"

Chocolate said, "Oh, yo sister run track? We could go watch her if y'all want."

We left the house around 2:30 p.m. and didn't get back from Mya's track meet until seven in the evening. Mya came in first place, so we took her out to eat. We didn't go anywhere fancy, just to a little Mexican restaurant called Jessica's.

As we ate, Mya commented about our pregnancies the whole time. Since she knew Chocolate was Charlie's sister, she didn't say anything out of the ordinary. She said stuff like, "I can't believe y'all is pregnant. Y'all should have at least waited. Shit, 'bout time I graduate from high school, y'all kids gone be two. I hope y'all baby daddies don't change up on y'all. Have y'all considered any names?"

Mya talked the whole time at the restaurant and the whole ride to the projects. We arrived at the projects in my Lexus, and I had Destiny's Child's CD blasting out of the speakers. I was playing their "Bills" song. All the bloods and hoodrats in the projects were like, 'Damn! That bitch got a Lexus.' I was showing off like, 'Yeah it's me'.

We dropped Mya off and headed home. When we arrived back in Hawthorne, Charlie was coming out of Chocolate's apartment with Joyce following him and smiling like a fool. My woman's intuition kicked in like, *why is my man coming out of this bitch's apartment?* I didn't say a word, because Joyce was Charlie's sister, and that was stupid of me to think.

However, Chocolate asked, "Joyce, where is my son? And what did you and Charlie just do? Y'all comin' outta my house smiling and shit."

I didn't know what to make of Chocolate's statement and question, but Charlie's smooth ass said, "Chocolate, we know you the oldest, but you can't have everything for yourself. If I decide to kick it with Joyce on my brother and sister day ma, don't get mad. Ya dig?"

Chocolate looked at Charlie with hate in her eyes, and said, "If I wasn't already spoiled, I'd trip!"

Mo'nique added, "I know that's right!"

I wasn't getting something. Their whole conversation was over my head and too much for me.

Charlie grabbed my hand and gave me a kiss. He said, "Shawty, where you been? Don't chu know I've been waiting on you for two hours? I got a surprise for you in the house."

I blurted. "Is that right?" I looked at the other girls and said, "I'll talk to y'all later."

They had envy written all over their faces, but I didn't care. Charlie was my man, not theirs.

My mouth hit the floor when I walked in my apartment. There was a brand new 150 gallon fish tank in my living room with over fifty tropical fish. I had told

Charlie I loved tropical fish two days after I moved in, and he told me he'd get me some.

I was elated at how he had the tank situated. With the lights off, my whole living room glowed blue. I knew Charlie had spent big money on my surprise, because the tank was custom made. Somehow, in the glass he had the company carve,

To my baby momma,

I love you...

Charles!

In the deep blue sea lies the seed of love and life. My mermaid, I love you with all my heart. Please, never forget this...

I was stunned. Charlie was turning all my dreams into reality. He was Mr. Perfect to me. Well, that was until I thought about the earlier phone call and spoiled the fun.

"Charlie, I'm sorry for spoiling yo surprise, but we need to talk."

"About what?" Charlie replied in a state of shock. I had changed up on him so fast he didn't know what hit him.

I said, "We need to talk about some bitch calling here telling me to tell you that Paul need some shoes and she need some money."

Charlie's eyes sprang wide open. He didn't say one word. I knew he was thinking of a way to cover his ass. Baby momma drama was written all over his face.

"Damn. Charlie, you lied to me! You lied to me!"

I got so loud it snapped him out of his trance. He said, "Shawty, calm down. It ain't what chu think. Paul is my boy. He's down right now, so I be sending him shoes and shit. I normally give his wife money to fly to Chicago to go see him, but if she's calling here disrespecting you, I'll cut that bitch off."

Charlie's explanation sounded valid to me. I even felt I was the one who answered the phone disrespectfully. "Naw, I think it was my fault we got off on the wrong foot. I answered the phone in an irritated tone. I'd gotten into it with my momma about my pregnancy a minute before she called. My mother hung up in my face, so when she called I answered with an attitude."

Just as I finished my statement, Charlie's phone went off. It always rang when we were in a serious debate or all the time. It was like he always got saved by the bell.

He answered, “Yo.”

“Aiyo, ma, I told chu about callin’ me with that bullshit. I told you to do what you gotta do. I’m already breakin’ more than enough bread, so what I care? You just hope everything go right, because if not, I want all mine back.”

“Is that right?”

“You not?”

“We’ll see!”

“Bye!”

Charlie’s whole demeanor had changed. When he hung up, I looked at him and he shook his head. Something was going on. I just couldn’t pinpoint it.

Charlie said, “Baby, life is getting too complicated. If it ain’t one thing, it’s the next. Living in these streets is a muthafucka. Shit just don’t go right!”

Charlie was pressed. Something was getting under his skin. Our whole little special moment was gone. The mood changed so fast, we forgot all about the fish tank.

I asked Charlie what was wrong and if he needed my help with anything. He got one call and it messed up the whole vibe.

"Daphne, as much as I wanna tell you my problems, I can't. It's just hard for me to vent my true emotions. I know I'm a complicated dude, but shit, nowadays life is complicated within itself."

Charlie was good at beating around the bush. I wanted to snap and say, "Charlie, just tell me the goddamn problem!"

However, I said, "Bae, everyone has his or her own struggles. You're not the only one with problems. I hope you don't think life is perfect, because it's not. I don't know what your problem is, but if you tell me, I might can help you. I know by sharing words and time, we deepen our roots, strengthen our relationship, and our foundations."

Charlie chuckled. I put a smile on his face. He was surprised by my wit and brilliance. He said, "Ma, I'm impressed with your wordplay, and your philosophy is quite amazing considering your age and occupation at this time."

I replied, "What chu thought, I didn't have nothing in my arsenal? I used to study the dictionary, if you didn't know. And before I moved in with you, I was receiving straight A's in school."

"Well, since you just said that, I'ma do you like my brother did me. We gonna put you in home studies, and for me, I want you to study ten words a day. This is how I got my high school diploma and twenty college units before I turned seventeen. I don't think you'll do like me, but if something go wrong, I don't need no dumb girl. Know what I mean?"

I knew Charlie wasn't the average street thug. All along, I knew he was book smart. We got along great because we had lot in common. I was street smart to a certain extent. He was street smart. I was book smart. I loved all the finer things life had to offer, and he stayed with all the finer things life had to offer. We were one of a kind.

I agreed to do home studies. He agreed to pay for it. We sat for hours talking. He told me after he handles all his business in the streets, we were moving out of the ghetto. I agreed with no hesitation.

It was 10 pm. when we got in bed. Charlie told me he had too much on his head to have sex, so I played with myself. Charlie had turned me into a nympho. I mean, I was once scared of the dick, but after being turned out by him I couldn't get enough of it. I believe that's how I became pregnant so fast.

As Charlie fell asleep, I started fingering myself. I wanted to strip him ass naked and hop on top of him, but I obeyed his commands. I let him sleep. At one in the morning, I had to go take a cold shower. My sex drive was at all-time high. My pregnancy had my hormones raging and they wouldn't let me sleep.

The next morning Charlie woke me up. He was he was in the bedroom cursing someone out. He was trying to whisper, but he was too heated to do so.

"Jessica, that bitch is crazy. She's getting on my last nerve!"

"Yeah, I heard from her last night. She said she ain't takin' shit. I told that janky ass bitch we'll see."

"Naw, I'm not gon' do nothing stupid. Im just gonna let you handle it. I've already went out asshole backwards fuckin' with dis bitch. Shit, I wish I could be like Mary J. Blige right now. I mean, a nigga don't need no mo' drama. Nowadays, I wish I never ran certain streets, because the streets coupled with busted ass bitches will drive a nigga crazy."

"So you talked to everybody else and they agreed?"

"Okay, that's cool! Make 'em do 'em all at separate times."

"Jess, I don't give a damn what Tracy and Charlene say. As long as they agree to our plan and don't come with no shit, I'll pay 'em whatever they want."

"Naw, don't worry about the four that's on the way, we'll do them later. Actually, we only gotta do three, because one is fo'sho."

"Oh yeah, what's the deal with the twins? Did she agree to that deal?"

"What chu mean, no? How is that bitch gon' act funny with mine? Yo, I swear these hoes act like they don't know they playin' with fire."

I lay in bed listening to Charlie talk to his sister-in-law for about an hour. I knew they were talking about business, but I was wondering who were these females they were talking about? The names were not familiar, so I knew they were talking about some out of state females.

I decided to stop ear hustling. I had to get up and do my chores around the house. Breakfast had to be made and I was late. My man needed his hot meal before he left the house.

I leapt out of bed, but was sidetracked when I saw Charlie's Hugo Boss pants and Timbo boots still lying on the floor. I wouldn't have been a woman if I didn't dig into his pockets. I didn't find anything out of the ordinary, so I marched my black insecure butt to the kitchen.

I ended up making some homemade waffles with sausage, grits, and eggs. When Charlie finally made it out of the bathroom smelling good, we ate and fed each other. We only had twenty minutes at our table, because Peewee and Black Dice were at the door as soon as we got started.

When I let them in, Peewee's loud mouth butt blurted, "Dayuuum, girl! Shit, I thought yo' ass was lyin' about bein' pregnant, but I see yo thick ass getting fat."

I rolled my eyes.

"Shit, you could roll yo' eyes all you want, but you betta hope you ain't one of them girls who be thick, then have a baby and become big as a house. Yeah, roll yo' eyes to dat."

Peewee started walking like a fat person while saying, "Hubba-hubba-hubba."

He was so comical even I had to laugh.

Then, I frowned. "Peewee, do you ever shut da hell up?"

"When it comes to you, no. Shit, you should be happy I like talkin' to you. If you were any other hoodrat I wouldn't be talkin' to you. I like yo' thick-fat-ass."

When Charlie and his boys left, I cleaned up, washed dishes, hopped in the tub, and fell back to sleep. I was tired. I needed some more sleep.

Chapter 6

Charlie

"Yo, I keep tellin' shawty to stop callin' my house and cell phone. I gave the phone number to y'all momma for her use, not Shondella's use."

I was forced by Shondella's foul play to take a suicidal chance. I had to go to her mother about all the drama she'd caused. However, my plan didn't go as expected. When my crew and I arrived, Shondella's brother, Rock Bottom, was out front with his homies.

I didn't know Rock Bottom from Adam. I knew he had just served a five-year bid for robbery and assault. He was supposed to have knocked out one of his homeboys and robbed him for $200. His homeboy turned around and told the law.

I was now face to face with Rock Bottom. He stood about six foot three. He and Black Dice were about the same height and size, so I wasn't trippin'. I introduced myself and he replied, "Oh, you the sucka-ass nigga who got my sister pregnant, huh?"

Rock Bottom was a Blood, so Bull chimed in. "A dawg, I'm Big Bull from Brimz and dis my folks. Blood ain't no square or no busta. Show some respect."

Rock Bottom looked Bull up and down. He saw that Bull was the same height and size as him, probably bigger. Bull's name wasn't Bull for nothing; he was a big black nigga.

Rock Bottom asked, "So who is these other niggas?"

Bunch chimed in. "Look, dawg, we only came to talk about yo' sister. She's doin' some uncalled for shit…"

As Bunch talked, I looked over my shoulder at Black Dice and Peewee. They were on guard like two Marines. Black Dice nodded to me as if to say, *Don't trip! I got dis nigga if he do anything outta line.* Dice had on a trench coat, with his Mack 10 strapped under it.

Peewee was the one I had to worry about. I knew when Rock Bottom asked, who is these other niggas?

Peewee wanted to say, "I'm Baby Peewee Loc from 39th Street, Harlem Crip!" However, I gave him a signal to let it slide.

Rock Bottom had five of his homeboys chillin' on his mother's porch with him. I thought, *cool, if anything goes wrong, it'll be an even fight. Six on six.* However, after Bunch finished talking, all hell broke loose.

I was telling Rock Bottom how I gave my house and cell phone numbers to his mother so she could call me when Paul needed something, but she gave the number to Shondella, and Shondella been calling my house and cell phone with all type of bullshit. I figured since Rock Bottom had been through baby momma drama with his baby momma, he'd be understanding. But to my surprise, as I spoke, he fumed. Then the devil herself pulled up with two of her homegirls.

"Aww hell naw! Y'all niggaz can leave my momma's house right now! Nobody asked fo' y'all niggaz to be all at my mom's house! And Charlie, I ain't takin' a DNA test either."

I frowned. "Why not? If you 100% sure like you say, a test shouldn't be a problem. Shit, I'm not mad dat you filin' for child-support."

I looked at Rock Bottom using my street smarts and asked, "Rock, did yo' sister tell you dat she was going to the people on me?"

I was playing mind games. I knew most street niggas hated the thought of knowing one of their folks were talking or messing with the folks. (The Law)

Rock Bottom looked puzzled. I was putting him on blast in front of his boys. He turned to Shondella. "Shondella, I know you ain't go to the people on dis nigga when momma told me he be shootin' you and her bread fo' Paul! Dis nigga probably ain't there physically for Paul, but, at least, he's doin' something!"

Shondella hated how I switched the script on her. I mean, I knew I couldn't win by arguing with her, so I let her brother do my dirty work. Shondella caught on to what I was doing and snapped.

Out of nowhere, Shondella slapped the shit out of me. I wanted to kill this bitch. I had to literally hold myself back, because I had never laid a hand on a woman. I fumed. Shit started moving fast.

"Nigga hit me!" she yelled. "You used to beat me when my brother was in jail. Beat me like you used to, you womanizer!"

I knew Shondella was a psychopath, but I didn't know she'd try to cross me like she did. "Look, ma, I know what you tryna do, so don't go there. You know a nigga never put a hand on you. And you know, outta all people, I don't deserve dat title."

Peewee snapped. "Charlie, fuck all dis bullshit! Let's just leave dis bitch house…"

Rock Bottom frowned, looked Peewee up and down, and cut him off. "Hol' on, nigga! Don't eva call my lil' sista a bitch."

He took a step toward Peewee, and Peewee screwed his face. "Nigga, what?"

I was trying to keep the drama down. I stepped in front of Rock Bottom so he and Peewee wouldn't clash. I said, "Yo, we didn't come here to start no shit."

Rock Bottom's boys all started reaching under their shirts, and he swung directly for my jaw. His punch landed between my right eyebrow and my temple. The punch was kind of hard and very unexpected. I hit the ground in a daze, and Shondella got exactly what she wanted.

Black Dice yelled, “Er’ body get tha fuck down!” I stayed on the ground and my crew ran for cover. The Bloods were caught off guard. They had guns, but when Black Dice pulled out his Mack 10, they started fumbling with theirs and running for cover. They took pop shots at him, but they didn’t know we all had on body armor. A few bullets bounced off his armor; that made Black Dice mad, and the only person who felt his wrath was Rock Bottom.

I watched Rock Bottom catch about thirty slugs. I looked at Shondella while we both lay flat on the ground, and she was screaming.

“Charlie, he’s killin’ my brotha! Stop him!”

I knew from the last time I took Dice to Harlem that it wasn’t a good idea to bother him when he’s in killing mode. I waited until he finished, and when he did, the sight was not nice. Rock Bottom was dead as a doorknob in a puddle of his own blood on his mother’s porch. Blood was even on me. I stood up and pulled out my gun.

I shot in the air five times and looked at Shondella. “Bitch, see what tha fuck you caused?”

She replied with tears streaming down her cheeks, "Aww, nigga, y'all killed my brotha! Y'all goin' to jail!"

Dice pointed his gun at Shondella. I grabbed his arm and said, "Naw homey, she gotta raise my son."

"Aiyo, lets bounce!" Maine called from the driver seat of my truck.

The whole team was in my truck, so I told Black Dice to hop in Maine's Benz and meet us at General Hospital. I hopped in the passenger seat of my truck and Maine smashed off. Dice turned the opposite way of us, and the Bloods started back taking pop shots. It was like they found some more ammunition when we were leaving.

As we rolled to East L.A., to General Hospital, I called Jessica. I knew my crew was about to take a loss, so I needed Jessica to have our lawyer meet me at Parker Center. When she answered, I told her what went down and she already knew what to do.

She said, "Charlie, you on a time limit. If it just happened, the police is just getting to the crime scene. Shondella gonna tell, so do all that you gotta do now. Have y'all story straight and make sure Dice has his head on straight before you do what y'all gotta do. I'll call you right back after I talk to Mr. Cooper."

When I hung up with Jessica, I told Peewee to call Black Dice. When Dice answered his phone, he said, "I'm right behind y'all."

We were now in East L.A. on a street called Eastlake. I told Maine to park in front of a little Mexican pharmacy.

"Peewee, tell Dice to park the Benz up the block, lock it up and come get in the truck with us. Also, Bull, you and Bunch go in that pharmacy and buy the strongest pain-killers on the shelf and two bottles of water."

When Bunch and Bull hopped out of the truck, Black Dice hopped in. He automatically said, "I'm ridin dis out."

It was as if he'd read my mind. After he killed Rock Bottom, I had to come up with a plan to clear his name. He was a real nigga, and my most loyal worker. This was the reason I shot five times in the air. From my understanding, Rock Bottom and his boys started firing on us, and then Dice pulled out his gun after getting shot by Rock Bottom.

I told Dice, "You gotta at least take two or three slugs, so I could get my lawyer to get you off this case."

Dice looked at me like, 'nigga are you crazy?' but didn't say a word, he just nodded. He knew the game, and he had to do whatever it took for us to keep him out of jail.

When Bull and Bunch came back with the painkillers and water, I told Dice to knock himself out. Maine drove to an alley two blocks away from the hospital and Dice and I hopped out.

"Aiyo, dis shit gonna hurt, but let's get dis over with. I'ma shoot one time in yo' shoulder and one time in each arm. That way, the people can't say you shot ya self."

Peewee hopped out of the truck and said, "Aiyo, kid, hol' on. Let's pray for the kid, Black Dice. Naw, shawty, I'm just playin'. I just hopped out to pick up the shells and give you dis infrared beam. Son, it won't be right if you shoot him at point blank range."

Peewee was trying to make light of the situation, but Dice wasn't going for it. "Peewee, cuzz, get yo' short ass back in the truck. Crip, a muthufucka bout ta get popped and you jokin' and shit..."

As Peewee did his job, Dice took his eyes off me. I faked like I was going to get something out of the truck, but turned around with the red beam and shot Dice in the shoulder. The bullshit penetrated through his right shoulder blade in and out.

He yelled, "Aww! Muthafucka you shot me!"

Peewee countered, "Aww nigga, dat wasn't shit! Nigga, yo' big-ass could take a lil' piece of metal."

Dice frowned. "Nigga, let me see you take one to the shoulder."

I fired again, twice.

"Cuuuuuuuuuuuzzzzzzz! Dat shit hurt."

Peewee and the whole team started laughing. I tried not to laugh, but Dice's reaction was too hilarious.

We were on a time limit, so I pulled myself together and said, "Alright homie, just one more."

Dice had never talked so much in his life until this day. Even when Peewee introduced us to each other when we were fourteen, I thought he had some kind of speech problem because he never talked.

As I took aim for my last shot, he said, "Nigga, I've already took three fo' yo New York ass, you best come on."

I shot again.

"Aww shit! Cuzz, I'm burnin'."

I doubled over in laughter. Dice was making a joke out of the whole ordeal. He started clowning. "I'm hit! I'm hit! I'm hit!"

We hopped back into the truck and Maine took off to the hospital. When we arrived, I told Dice to make sure he told the doctors he went to Shondella's momma's house with me, and Rock Bottom, Shondella's gang member brother shot him.

I said, "Dice, make sure you tell the doctors to call the police. Tell them that you were protecting yourself and you think you killed one of the gang members with your gun. Do not tell them that you're a gang member. Tell them you work at a restaurant called Jessica's. Shondella probably tellin' er' thang, except that she started it, so if the police start asking way out questions, fake like you are in too much pain to talk. Our lawyer will have er' thang under control as soon as I talk to him. Police will probably charge you with murder off top. But if you go in there and sell it to these people like you're innocent, the doctors will help you beat the case by self-defense. I saw my brother do dis same shit before, so I know it works. The only bad thing is you might have to spend a few nights in jail until we can bail you out."

Dice nodded and hopped out the truck.

Peewee said, "Nigga, you best go play yo' role and win an Oscar, or that'll be yo' ass, Smokey."

We watched Dice as he walked in the hospital and collapsed. We all started dying. The scene looked like something out of a movie, but this was real life.

Jessica called me two hours after we dropped Dice off at the hospital. The team and I went straight to our honeycomb hideout. Our honeycomb hideout was in the city of Carson. It was a small shack that sat on some property Peewee bought for his mother after he made his first million. His mother's house sat in the front and the shack was in the back. The hideout was a spot we plushed out with two PlayStations and two 62-inch televisions. It was only built to keep us occupied while we lay low.

When Jessica called, I was in the living room with my team going over our story. I had to make sure we were all under the same storyline. I answered my phone and Jessica said, "Choo, Jay Cooper will be in front of Parker Center waiting on you in an hour. I will be there too. But what do you need me to do in between time, because I swear I wanna kill yo' triflin' ass baby momma myself."

I told Jessica to have one of her workers put us on her payroll. She agreed.

"Choo, you got me so stressed. I mean, I hate that you just put yo' dick in anybody. It's crazy, because I don't think I know anybody your age as smart as you, but then again, I don't know anybody who is as dumb as you either."

Okay, it was time to go. I didn't need to hear Jessica get on me. I wasn't in the mood. The only thing I was thinking about was how I could beat this murder without coming in contact with the law. There was actually no way around it.

"Also, Choo, before I go, I want to tell you that Maria agreed to let the twins come stay with you for a few weeks. However, I'ma call her later and tell her we got to reschedule. We do not need them kids out here while you going through this."

I was damned. I was a poor excuse for a man. Life was throwing all kinds of wrenches in the game. I was getting hit with low blows from left to right. These women I played in my past were coming back to haunt me like ghosts. I was being hunted from coast to coast. What a nightmare.

When I hung up with Jessica, I slammed my fist into my palm and yelled, "Fuck! I hate life!"

"Yo, B, what's wrong witchu?" Maine asked. "Are we straight or what? You shoulda let Dice kill dat bitch, B."

"Maine, please!" I yelled. "Just shut tha fuck up!"

I was flipping out. It felt like everything and everybody was bothering me. I needed to get away from all the bullshit and isolate myself. I grabbed the keys to Peewee's Lincoln Town Car and said, "I'll be back."

I took the 91 freeway on Avalon to the I-110. When I got to the I-110, I had all four windows rolled down in Peewee's Town Car. His car was the hottest in Cali and it had an Alpine system that was killing the game, but I kept the music off. The only sound I wanted to hear was my thoughts and the wind blowing by.

I arrived at Parker Center, LAPD headquarters, and realized that I had made a critical mistake. My dumb ass still had on the white T-shirt that I had on when Rock Bottom got killed, and it had blood on it. However, in the trunk, Peewee kept two to three brand new Pro Clubs. I slid out of the bloody T-shirt and slid in one of Peewee's.

"Hey, young man!" Jay Cooper said, scaring the shit out of me. "You're supposed to have done that at home."

I shook my head. "Yo, I was slippin'."

"I see. Didn't your brother teach you that we, L.A. brothers are creepers? We watch everything."

"Come on, Jay! In the N-Y we know how to creep too. I just slipped and almost just fell. My head is all fucked up. Dis street shit is killin' me."

"Well, let's go sign in. The less time we take to sign in, the better. They wouldn't be able to say you didn't come straight to them. You can tell me what's what while we're waiting to see a detective."

I loved Jay Cooper. He was the only black lawyer other than Johnny Cochran who stayed on the grind for his folks that I knew of. His ghetto pass was valid in every hood in California. Niggas knew Jay from L.A. to the Bay. E represented over twenty high profile cases and had a record of 20 and 1. His only loss came from the infamous Crip, Killa Black, and LAPD had already pegged him.

After Jay Cooper and I signed in, we were told to have a seat because we had to see the regional homicide detective, and that it would take no less than an hour. We agreed and walked out of the police headquarters. We walked back to Peewee's Town Car and sat on the hood talking. I was wondering where he parked. I parked right in front of the headquarters and put five dollars' worth of quarters in the meter.

I asked, "Hey! Bruh, where did you park? Because I don't see your car and Jessica is nowhere to be found."

Jay chuckled. "See, Mr. Warner, when you get the credentials I got, you can park anywhere you want. I didn't want to take a chance at getting my brand new

Caddy broken into on these mean streets of L.A., so I parked in the police garage. I parked in the lieutenant's parking spot, but when he sees my plates, he'll find somewhere else to park."

I smiled. "Big pimpin', huh?"

"Naw, what I'm saying is, when you get yourself together and learn how to put a suit and tie on, you'll see how people actually fear a black man in a suit and tie more than brothers in that thug attire."

I had on Peewee's plain white Pro Club T-shirt, some dark blue 501 pants, and some crispy white Reebok Classics. Jay Cooper had on an all black three-piece Armani suit, a white button down shirt, a black Italian made tie, and some shining white gators. As Jay talked, I realized what he was saying was true. Parker Center had traffic in and out of it all night, and every person who walked by acknowledged Jay and looked at me as if I was shit, and these were street oriented people. I guess they thought I was talking to the people or telling on someone.

"Charlie, when you get home tonight, give my theory some thought. However, right now, I need to know everything that actually occurred. Then, I wanna hear your side of the story."

I started explaining what happened. I told Jay how Shondella was following us and almost got killed. I told him how she stayed wasting my money on herself instead of my son. How I started taking money to her mother for Paul. How I gave her mother my number and she gave it to Shondella. How Shondella called Daphne and almost got me caught up. How she threatened to file child-support, but didn't want to take a paternity test.

"Yeah, Jay, all this shit started over some baby momma drama. I went to her mom's house to confront her about puttin' me through so much bullshit for nothing. But when I got over there, Shondella's jailbird brother was outta jail. A lil' confrontation happened, but everything was under control until Shondella arrived. She came and made up some story about how I used to beat her when her brother was in jail. She slapped me two times to try to get me to flip my wig, but I didn't. All went bad when one of my boys realized what she was tryna do. He said, 'Charlie, let's leave this bitch house,' and her brother snapped. He and my boy was 'bout to get into it, so I jumped between them. I didn't need no more problems, but her brother dope fiended me with a power punch. He hit me so hard, I was sleep before I hit the ground. His five homeboys at the house with him started reaching for their pistols. My boy on my team immediately drew heat. He laid everything down with his Mac-10. The Bloods shot back, but we had on vests. Shondella's brother ended up gettin' killed. Afterwards, my boy told Shondella the shootout was all her fault."

Jay stood in silence while I talked. I guess he was trying to visualize everything that took place. When I finished telling him the actual story, he said, "Man, you young brothers gonna learn the hard way. Y'all steady gettin' these young girls pregnant and don't look at the flip side. It's brothers serving years in prison because their baby mommas got them locked up on some false allegations. Domestic violence and drug cases are the two leading causes for black men being the majority in prisons. Anyhow, I'm glad you fired five times in the air. I see your brother did teach you something before he passed. I'm proud of you! I don't need to hear your side of the story. I just need to know who's in the hospital, where he got hit, and where's his machine gun? Also, if this regional homicide detective ask why did your buddy bring a pistol with him if y'all didn't go over there to start no trouble, tell him Rock Bottom or whatever his name is, made multiple death threats on you and your boys' lives from jail over the phone. Say that your friend only brought the gun because Rock Bottom was a known gang member."

I agreed and we walked back into Parker Center. Jessica was still nowhere to be found. I was starting to worry about her. It wasn't her character to miss something as important as a murder case. She was my number one fan.

Before Jay Cooper and I went to see the homicide detective, I called her. I needed to make sure nothing had happened to her on her way to Park Center. Shit, with the way my luck was going, I was worried shitless. She could have gotten into an accident or something.

When I picked up my cell phone, I realized I had turned it off when I left the honeycomb. Forgot I didn't want to be bothered. My message light was flashing. I ignored it and dialed Jessica's cell phone. She answered on the first ring.

"Boy, don't neva have me scared like this! I've been calling your phone for the last hour. With all this shit going on right now, don't neva turn off yo' phone. Have you talked to the detective yet?"

"No."

"Well, I'm still comin' up there. I just picked up Momma from the airport. We're coming straight there."

I thought, *damn! Is she talkin' bout my momma? She didn't tell me my crackhead-ass momma was comin' out here.*

"Who you talkin' bout, my momma?"

"Who else, Choo?"

Silence. I didn't reply. I had heated passion for my mother. I hated the way she just neglected my brother and I for crack. Even though she was now clean, I still held a grudge against her.

"Choo, I know how you feel about Momma, but we're all human. If JR forgave her before he passed, you can too. Anyhow, we'll talk later. I'm on my way."

By the time Jessica and my mother made it to Parker Center, the talk with the regional homicide detective was over. It only lasted 45 minutes, which surprised me. The regional homicide detective's name was Julius Henson. Surprisingly, he was a well-dressed middle-aged black man, who Jay Copper knew very well.

Jay Cooper told him I was one of his top clients and that he had watched me grow up. Julius' eyes lit up when Jay Cooper told him he watched me grow up. I guess that was some kind of code to him, because the first question he asked was, "Is all expenses paid?"

I looked at Jay Cooper. He smirked and said, "Answer the question."

I knew my attorney was top notch and connected, but I didn't know he had lead detectives in L.A. working for him. It was like some high powered, professional, illegal/legal shit taking place. I instantly learned from the two professional men that it pays to know the laws and how to break them.

I replied, "All expenses paid with a ten percent bonus if you make sure that the case is never opened and that me and my boy, Roger Lee, and the rest of my crew don't get put on the LAPD watch list."

"That's a lot to ask for on the first go around, but if the money is right, I can see what I can do."

Julius Henson was more of a businessman than detective. Money wasn't a thing to me. I thought, *man, we need more people like this working as detectives; less black men would be in jail.*

I knew most people in the professional world believed in the saying, 'money talks, bullshit walks,' so I used my best business approach.

"Look, bruh! By no means was this a premeditated murder. My boy was protecting himself and our crew. However, I hate bullshit, so let's make this money talk and this bullshit walk. I got $100,000 plus ten percent bonus when I get the papers that the case won't be opened. Also, Rock Bottom was a reputable gang member in the Blood community. I know how much LAPD dislikes gang members. I mean, they're killing our people and they don't care."

Julius Henson looked at Jay Cooper and said, "Jay, this young punk must think I'm new to this, huh?"

Jay Cooper threw his hands in the air. He didn't say one word, making a gesture as if to say, 'I'm not in it'.

"Young brotha, let me tell you something. This might be a little too personal and a low blow, but take it for what it's worth. I hate young brothas like you more than I hate the Crips and Bloods. I hate the fact that someone took the time to educate you, and you're very smart, but you're also dumb. See, I hate brothas like you because you know right from wrong. A lot of Crips, Bloods, and other thugs don't understand a left shoe from a right shoe. Many of these people can't spell dog, and the ones who do aren't doing nothing with themselves. I say out of every hundred, only eight will have a high school diploma. Out of that eight percent, only one or two will enter a college. So it's brothers like you who got laced pretty good on how to run an organization, but can't, because you can't control the small things like your small head."

I knew Julius Henson was spitting some real knowledge. I thought, *nigga, you should be a reverend or something,* but I didn't say a word. He kept going.

"See, what I'm talking about is this new movement in the black community of big pimpin', booty poppin', bootylicious, and all that other stuff. Brothas aren't living up to the dream Dr. King had. The dream wasn't for brothas and sistas to promote genocide forty years later. What I'm getting at is, brothas are brainwashed. You young guys think y'all can just go in any sista without any protection. You guys don't think of the consequences, so 'bout time y'all commit the crime, a child is conceived or a disease is transmitted. The young women out there aren't as strong as they used to be, so they open their legs to damn near anybody."

Julius Henson had switched from the matter at hand and turned into an activist. I looked at Jay Cooper, and all he did was smile. He even instigated.

"Charles, tell Mr. Henson how old you are and how many kids you got."

I told Julius Henson my age, how many baby mommas I had, and my child count. He blurted, "Holy shit! Five, and four on the way?"

I nodded.

"See, that's why I'm trying to talk some sense into your head. Man, the route you're going only ends in pain and remorse down the line. Take my words wisely. I'm an old dog. I roamed the same streets as you, and it wasn't what I thought it was going to be at the end. And to sum my lecture up, over the last few years I've been conducting a survey. I've been counting all the people that come through this L.A. County booking system with AIDS. My survey concludes that us black folks are in trouble, and due to my survey, I recommend that you go take an AIDS test and slow yourself down. I know if Cooper is representing you, you're a boss at what you're doing, so I know you got women flopping to their knees. However, you got to start resisting temptation. These women will get you in a lot of trouble. I humbly advise you to find that right young sista or woman and settle down. Set a foundation and take it from there. Anyhow, let's get back to business."

I said, *Thank you Jesus* to myself and stayed quiet.

"Look, young brotha, I've been doing this for years. I've even did business with your brother, and if Jessica and Jay didn't call me immediately, I wouldn't take a chance on messing with you. See, JR played ball with my son, so he was like my son. I've already got the job done on this case. Homicide at Rampart Station will be sending me their murder book on this Mr. Moore case. As soon as everything comes in, I will have the case forwarded to me. However, $100,000 won't even pay off my foot soldiers. I need at least, a million dollars and my ten percent bonus. I will get the case by the morning and your boy will not be arraigned. Detectives have already filed the case as manslaughter. Your boy is under arrest at L-A-G-H. He's been treated at the hospital for multiple gunshot wounds. Also, I like how you shot him twice in the same spot. That was smart. An average detective would never think twice about him shooting himself. They say he played his role so righteously the doctors were terrified. They say the doctors reported that your friend was ambushed and acted in self-defense. I just received word on the case right before you guys walked in, so if you want this bullshit to end today and your boy to be freed by tomorrow, I will need at least $1.1 million in total."

I shook my head. Julius Henson was on top of his game like Michael Jordan in the 80s and 90s. He knew who I was and all about the case before I even walked in. I was more in awe that my brother was so connected. At that moment, I realized how powerful I was and that the saying, "it ain't who you are, it's who you know," is very true.

I agreed to pay Mr. Henson $1.1 million, and he said, "Everything will be resolved within 72 hours. Deliver the money to Jay. He'll know what to do with it."

I smiled. "Done deal."

I was taking a big loss because of my baby momma drama, but I had to be happy. Dice wasn't going to do jail time. I pledged at that very moment to settle down. I started thinking over my life and contemplating marriage.

Chapter 7

Daphne

Some strange stuff had been happening, but I just couldn't pinpoint the issue. I was five months pregnant, big as a house, and starting to be insecure because of my weight. Charlie was doing stuff he never did before. One day, he came home with a black eye after staying out all night. I asked him what happened. He said, "I got into it with some niggaz."

I asked, "Over what?"

He stuttered, "Over… over some bitch!"

I snapped, "Over some bitch? What bitch?"

He frowned. "Naw-Naw! Over some bitch shit. I told you how these Cali niggaz be hatin'."

"Charlie, why would some niggaz just be hatin' on you? You don't gangbang, and you stay with four reputable gangbangers. Shit, are you sleeping with some other nigga's girl or something? Because you did stay out all night, and that's the only way I see some niggaz out here giving you a black eye."

Charlie frowned. "Yo, shawty, I told you about questioning me like the Feds. I got a muthafuckin black eye and you don't even care! You worryin' bout is I'm cheatin'. I told you, you my only girl, so leave me the fuck alone with your insecurities."

Charlie was right. I was insecure. I left the conversation alone, walked to the kitchen and made him an ice pack. After I gave him his ice pack, I went to run his bath water.

When he got in the tub, I got in with him. He started washing my belly with a warm washcloth. He kissed it and said, "I know this one is mine right here."

I wanted to ask, "Nigga, what do you mean by dat?" but I stayed quiet. I was loving the way he was caressing my body, and I didn't want the feeling to end.

He whispered, "Ma, our son gon' be big, because you are super big. Shit, you might be having twins."

Just as Charlie's caresses started getting intense, his phone rang. He stopped dead in his tracks, hopped out of the tub, ran to our room, and blurted, "Hello!" into his phone.

I stayed in the tub thinking he was going to come right back, but I was wrong. He started arguing with some female named Maria, and I heard everything.

"Look, Maria! They can come out here any time you want them to, but don't make it seem like I'm the one bullshitin' when you know damn well that I can't come back dat way until things cool down."

"Yeah, ma you right! They do need me, but you ain't workin' with me. I'm starting to think you're against me. I had Jessica give you my phone number so we could work dis out and not get into it. I mean, either you gonna work with me or against me. Maria, you can't have it your way. Either you on my team or I don't need you. I'll just have to accept the fact that I made a terrible mistake."

"No. I'm not sayin' it like dat, but shit, if we can't come to an agreement, I might as well keep having Gotti do what he's doing."

"Maria, dat ain't a question. You family. You know I'm gon' have love for you 'til death do us part."

What? I thought. *I can't believe dis. Dis nigga is talkin' to dis bitch like they fuckin' or somethin'. Dis nigga best not be playin' me!*

I immediately hopped out of the tub to confront him while Maria was on the phone, but bout time my big-ass made it to the room he was hanging up.

"Like dat, Charlie?"

"Ma, what are you talkin' bout now?"

"Nigga, you know what I'm talkin' bout! You don't even take into consideration dat I was in the house! You just tell a bitch you gonna love her 'til death do y'all part like I'm not even here!"

Tears flooded my eyes. I was hurt. For the first time in my life, I felt less than a woman. Charlie was playing me like dominoes, I just knew it. My gut feeling was telling me. However, I was in love and needed to hear him talk his way out of it.

"Daphne, ma, what's the deal? Is yo' pregnancy gettin' the best of you? I know you done got big, but baby you my true love. You know I deal with a lot of different broads. I keep a bitch on my team, and I love every broad that don't mind puttin' some money in our pocket. It's not the same love we share, but it's love. Like a homie love."

"So if you don't love her like you say you love me, why is dis my first time hearing of her?"

Charlie just shook his head and started drying off. He ignored my question as he put on his under clothes. With him ignoring me, the dagger in my heart traveled deeper within. Silence kills me. I snapped.

"Charlie, you best tell me something!"

I was crying a river. He put on his pants and said, "Look! You know I love you, but I love my family too. They are the people who are gonna ride with me! So, if I tell a woman in our family I love her, it's not the way I love you. I told you when we first got together I have a family in mostly every state, so once again, work with me not against me!"

I wanted to say, "Nigga, you just told Maria that same catch phrase."

"Go get dressed!" he said, interrupting my thoughts. "You're going with me today. I wanted to show you it ain't what you think it is. So while you get dressed, I'm 'bout to walk to Chocolate's unit. I gotta holla at her. Peewee should be here within thirty minutes, so wear something nice. I'm taking you to meet my moms. She's out here visiting Jessica.

Peewee arrived at around 11:30 am and Charlie was still at Chocolate's. I invited him in, surprised that he was by himself. I immediately asked, "Where's Dice?"

He shook his head. "Didn't Charlie tell yo' fat ass about askin' so many questions?"

I was starting to hate Peewee. He was one of those people you hate one minute, then love the next. He was a real L.A. nigga. Being around him and Charlie taught me the difference between an East Coast nigga and a West Coast nigga.

To me, niggas on the East Coast were sensitive, while niggas on the West Coast stayed portraying the hardcore role. Niggas on the West Coast only worried about the red and blue while niggas on the East Coast worried about blackness and getting money. The only thing I realized was the same between niggas from each coast was they love money, cars, clothes, bling-bling and women.

When Charlie came back from Chocolate's apartment, he was smiling and his shirt was wrinkled. I'd just ironed his shirt before he left. I fumed.

"Charlie, how did yo' shirt get wrinkled so fast!"

Charlie shook his head. I don't know what he was thinking, but he surprisingly said, "What chu talkin' bout?"

I screwed my face. "Nigga, I'm talkin' about yo' shirt!"

Peewee understood me well. He chimed in. "Man, just take off yo' shirt so she could re-iron it. Tell her you were down there playin' with yo' nephew."

I glanced at Peewee and cut my eyes. "Big Mouth, I wasn't talkin' to you."

"And I wasn't talkin to you." Peewee gave me the evil eye. "And I told you about rolling yo' eyes at me. One day them bitches gon get stuck and I'ma laugh at yo' fat ass."

Peewee knew how to get on a woman's nerves. He wasn't an ugly guy, but at times, I wondered if he had a girlfriend. As much as he got on my nerves, I couldn't imagine him with anyone. He was one of them niggas most bitches would say was fine, but once they got to know him, they would say he's too arrogant and cocky.

I ended up ironing Charlie's shirt again while he and Peewee stood in the living room talking. As I ironed his shirt, I smelled Chocolate's strawberry Victoria Secret's body spray that she wore daily. I didn't think anything of it. I let it go and started listening to them talk. They were in the living room. I was in the bedroom.

"Homie, why you didn't come back to the honeycomb last night? You turned yo' phone off like you didn't wanna be bothered, so Maine, Bull and Bunch went O.T."

"Damn!" Charlie blurted." "How much work did they take?"

"I think they had ol' girl from upstairs ship them two keys dis morning."

"Yo, dis nigga Maine is getting too loose. I told dat nigga stop flyin' back and forth. These Feds gon' grab a hold to his ass and it ain't gon' be nothin' nice. Do you remember Gotti B from Harlem?"

"Yeah. Dat was young cuzz who rode with me to scope out them Ricans. I like lil' cuzz. What, he's about sixteen now?"

"Yeah, that's him."

"Well, I'm thinkin' about givin' him Maine's position and lettin' Maine have the East Coast. With Gotti just sittin' around doin nothin', that will make him appear to be in a higher position than Maine. Gotti B is a good leader and listener. Maine lacks these two valuable qualities."

"Well, bruh, I don't know what to tell you. But you do gotta get at cuzz and tell him. He's tryna run his own program and it's not cool. But on the real, we tried to call you before they left, so it might not be their fault. I think they went down south. You know Maine is in love with dat bitch from Miami. I believe that's where they went."

"Anywayz, Crip, what's the business on dat case? You get it taken care of?"

"Yo, I almost forgot. Come help me load up some duffle bags."

As I ear hustled, Charlie and Peewee walked into the room that Charlie kept locked. After they entered, Charlie called for me to come to the room. I was all smiles when I entered the second room. It was plushed out with two leather couches, a big screen TV, a blue tinted light bulb, and a two hundred and fifty gallon fish tank with a baby shark in it. Posters of famous civil rights activists, Malcom X, Dr. King, George Jackson and Jesse Jackson were on each wall.

"Daphne, dis the room, I s'pose to be surprisin' you with. So..."

"Hol' on!" Peewee cut Charlie off. They were up to no good because they were chuckling. "Hol' on, Charlie. I got a deal for fat girl. Daphne, for you to get what my boy about to give you, you gotta..."

Peewee paused. He went into his jeans pocket and pulled out a quarter. He then tossed it into the tank.

"Now, fat-ass, back to what I was sayin'. To get yo' surprise, you gotta reach yo' hand in dat tank and grab dat quarta."

I looked at the fish tank and saw the shark swimming back and forth like he was just waiting to eat something up, and it wasn't about to be my hand. I blurted, "Hell naw! Nigga, I don't think whateva surprise y'all got is worth me losin' my hand."

"I know that's right, ma, "Charlie agreed. "Especially with what I got for you."

I turned toward Charlie with my hands on my hips and asked, "Charlie, what do you got? I ain't got time to be playin' these lil' games with you and yo' psycho ass homeboy?"

As soon as I finished my question, Charlie's cell phone went off. That nigga was Mr. Important. His cell phone rang like he was a 9-1-1 dispatcher. He looked at the incoming call, shook his head, and didn't answer.

Peewee's phone went off. next He answered, "What's crackin'?"

"Yeah. We're on our way. We just gotta load up some shit. We'll be there in a minute."

Peewee hung up his phone and said, "Cuzz, we gotta go get the homie. The hospital cleared him."

When Peewee stated that, I immediately knew Charlie wasn't lying about getting into it with some other dudes. I also knew Dice had gotten shot. No wonder Peewee didn't want to tell me where Dice was.

As I put two and two together in my head, Charlie said, "Daphne, take down dat Malcom X poster from the wall. You'll see a safe after you do that. The combination is your date of birth. When you get it open, read the card while Peewee and I count dis money over here."

I did as told and couldn't believe my eyes when I opened the safe. In front of a stack of money sat a diamond ring that I knew only celebrities wear during award shows.

"Oh my God! Charlie, thank you sooo much."

I was so elated I didn't realize Charlie and Peewee had taken down all the other posters in the room and opened three other duffle bags. I'd never seen so much money in my life. It looked like Charlie and Peewee had just robbed a bank.

"Daphne, stop lookin' at us. You need to read that card under that ring case, and tell me what you think."

Charlie was so cordial, I did exactly as told. I turned my focus back on the ring. I didn't think about the money. The ring looked to have more value. I grabbed the small Hallmark card from underneath the ring and it read,

Black Women

When brothers fall, our sisters stand tall.

These women are the strongest, because

they have been through it all.

They know the struggles we live, and strengthen

their lives so they can give.

They are smart, unique, and pure.

They pride themselves on their nappy hair

and mahogany skin.

They will fight you, punch you, and kick you.

Then they will feed you, hug you, and love you.

Black women are sometimes complicated,

but that's black women.

And I love my black women!

Daphne Johnson, will you marry me?

Oh my God! No he didn't! Charlie was actually asking me to marry him. I was surprised. He was making a dream come true. My father never asked my mother to marry him, so I was doing better than she was, I thought.

I felt tears rush to my eyes and my stomach started to turn. I was so happy that I felt sick. I had to throw up. Our baby was even elated.

I ran to the bathroom and scared the shit out of Charlie. I leaned over the toilet with my face buried in the bowl and gave up half of my intestines.

"Yo, ma, are you alright? It looks like my question was too much for you."

Peewee added, "Nigga, it wasn't too much for her. She's a big girl. I mean, look at her big-ass. She just been eatin' too fuckin' much. The baby got tired of being stuffed and started actin' a fool. Naw, though, you all right, fat-ass?"

"Yes."

"Well, get yo' fat-ass together and let's get ready to go."

Peewee was a pest at times, but I did like his sense of humor.

After I brushed my teeth and washed my mouth, I walked back into the room. I answered Charlie's proposal by saying, "Charlie, I love you. You are my baby daddy. I will marry you any time."

He replied, "A nigga can't ask for nothing more. We'll wait until you turn eighteen. That'll give us enough time to get everything we need together. However, I need you to study that poem and understand every word, because there'll be times you'll need to ride with me. There'll be times when life will feel like it's not worth living. And there'll be times we'll have to climb steep mountains. But I ask of you as a beautiful, intelligent, young black woman to marry me, because I know that you are strong and you are the one."

"Cuzz, you gon' make me cry with dat heartwrenching bullshit. Boo-hoo-boo-hoo! Nigga, lets finish what we gotta do and get going. Y'all can tell each other how much y'all love each other later. Let's finish counting dis money and get ghost. Shit, Daphne still haven't taken the money out of her safe."

Peewee was now talking over my head. Charlie didn't tell me to touch the money in my safe. I looked at both of them and asked, “What am I supposed to do with all that money.”

At age fifteen, $100,000 stuffed in a safe looked like a few millions to me.

Charlie replied, “Since you like doing hair, I’m taking you to meet my sister-in-law so she could help you open yo’ own salon. But you still gotta complete yo’ home study classes first.”

I agreed. Things were moving fast. I was being spoiled, and Charlie was turning into my everything.

After Charlie loaded a total of five duffle bags in his truck, which Peewee was driving, he hopped in my Lexus. He told me to drive right behind Peewee. He didn’t want anyone to be able to hop behind Peewee in traffic, so I stayed on his bumper.

As we rode, Charlie reclined the passenger seat all the way back. He stayed quiet the whole ride, but his phone didn’t. Every time it went off, he hissed, “Man, I can’t wait to see the results. Man, I pray to God…”

Charlie was going through it. Something and someone was really bothering him. As his woman, I had to ask what was wrong.

He simply replied, "Nothing."

I knew he was lying.

I said, "Charlie, you just asked me to marry you, but you can't even talk to me about the things that have been bothering you. For us to make it, we gonna have to learn how to confide in each other."

"Daphne, please! I got a headache right now. I'm going through a lotta shit and don't need to bring you into my drama. I know I asked you to be my wife, but I gotta get over dis on my own. Just know one thing, the things I did to make me smile are now making me cry. Daphne, I'm all fucked up in the head right now. Ma, just fall back."

Charlie was becoming very difficult to deal with. He was the man I've always wanted, but I was seeing that he had issues. One minute he was easy to get along with, then the next he was a complete asshole. It was like he was hiding something from me or doing some kind of dope on the under. He was low-key driving me crazy.

I screwed my face. "Charlie, I'm not stupid. I know you are hiding somethin' from me! You might as well be a man and come clean. Just get it off yo' chest. I know it's somethin', because er' time yo' phone ring, you look at the number then at me. You don't answer, but start cursin' yo' self. Somethin' is up. You done gave yo' self up."

"Naw, for real doe, "Charlie said with a stone face. "First, we gotta pickup Maine's ride, hopefully no crackhead broke into it. Then we can handle dat other stuff."

His phone rang again, and this time he anaswered.

"Yo."

"All right."

"Yeah."

"All right. One."

When Charlie hung up, he looked at me. "Peewee bout to pull up in front of Maine's ride. You pull next to it. I'm bout to hop in the truck. Follow me, all right?"

I nodded and cut my eyes at the same time. "Charlie, you are not off the hook, so don't dare think that you are."

Within seconds, Charlie was in Maine's Benz trailing Peewee while I trailed him. I knew he was relieved to be out of the car with me. He was on his cell phone again! He wasn't talking to Peewee, because we were now at General Hospital and Peewee was out the truck acting like he was wiping the rims.

Everything was planned, because as soon as Black Dice walked past Peewee in a hospital gown, Peewee dropped an Old Navy bag by the tire. Dice picked it up, hopped in the car with Charlie, and Peewee hopped back into Maine's car. Charlie kept talking on his phone while Dice stripped out of that hospital gown.

From the position I had taken, I could see that Black Dice had gotten shot in the shoulder blade and in both arms. He was patched and bandaged in each wounded area. Sorrow filled my heart. I'd never known anyone who'd been shot. In the projects, people got shot left and right. However, none of them were people I knew or had any concern with.

I watched Black Dice as he got dressed in some Phat Farm clothes. His hair was freshly braided, so I guess one of his family members or one of his girlfriends came to visit him, because this was the first time in months he had someone do something with his hair. He had it in crisscross cornrows to the back.

When he got dressed, Charlie hung up his phone and gave him dap. They shared a laugh about something, and Charlie gave Peewee the signal to go. We started back in our three-car processional, and I followed Charlie while listening to my Destiny's Child CD.

Ten minutes later, we arrived at Jessica's mansion looking house, and I became nervous. Charlie spoke highly of Jessica. I didn't know what she'd think of me. Not only was I meeting Jessica, I was also meeting his mother.

I looked in my rearview mirror to make sure I was looking half-decent, but for the first time during my pregnancy, I realized that my face had blown up. My pretty face was gone! I looked like a whale and a whole different person. I wanted to cry. I'd never been fat a day in my life. Even though I was pregnant, I was losing all my self-esteem.

As I looked in the mirror, Charlie came and opened my door. "Come on, shawty, you look good. Don't worry."

I replied, "No I don't! Peewee is right. I'm as big as a house."

"Daphne, that's because you're pregnant. Come on now, don't start doubting yo' pretty self now."

"Charlie, it's yo' fault! You the one who nutted in me."

Charlie cracked a smile. "Ma, you sho' is takin' dis pregnancy hard, ain't chu?"

I nodded. "Yep."

We made it to Jessica's house at around 2:30 in the afternoon, and it was 6 o'clock before I finally felt relaxed around Miss. Warner and Jessica. The first hour I sat talking to Miss Warner, because Charlie, Peewee, Jessica, and Black Dice were sitting in the kitchen counting money. Miss Warner and I sat in the living room getting to know each other.

She said, "Daphne, I haven't been there for my son like I was supposed to, but I'm a hundred percent sure he loves you. You the first girl I heard he actually lived in a house with. When I was sprung off dope, Charlie used to be a little player. Girls used to come looking for me just to ask where's my son was. I've already added you to the family. I know it's something about you that got Charlie stuck. Girl, I can tell you ain't going anywhere."

I smiled. "I hope not, because he did just ask me to marry him."

The living room and kitchen were right next to each other, so Charlie heard my comment and saw me flashing my engagement ring to his mother.

"Momma, that's only if she's willin' to ride with me through thick and thin. Because even though she knows the life I live, she don't! I be tryna tell her, the streets are a muthafucka, but she don't understand."

Miss Warner added, "Yeah, baby, them streets are something terrible, especially to someone who's caught up in them. I take all the blame for the pain and suffering Charles goes through. I mean, the streets can ruin the best of people. Daphne, I've spent over twenty years on and off the streets before finally realizing that I destroyed my family. And those twenty years were the worst of my life. At times, my past comes back and haunts me because I made mistakes. My worst mistake is leaving my two sons for crack. If I wasn't sprung off dope, my oldest son probably wouldn't be dead. He'd probably be in the NFL..."

Tears flooded Miss Warner's eyes then rolled down her cheeks in rivers. I felt her pain. She felt it was her fault JR was dead. Plus, she hated the fact that Charlie was hesitant about forgiving her. I wanted to just hug Miss Warner and tell her it's going to be alright, but Jessica beat me to it.

She stopped what she was doing and came into the living room. "Momma, I told you, it ain't yo' fault JR is dead. And when Choo-Choo comes around to finding himself, he'll accept you and forgive your mistakes. This is why you came to stay with me. We need to get our family back together. My daughters need their grandma, and Choo's kids gon' need you too."

Kids! I thought. My whole demeanor changed. *Is dis bitch insinuating that Charlie already got kids?*

Jessica must have sensed my antennas going up, because she then said, "I mean your kids, Daphne."

I forced a smile. I was starting to really like Jessica. She was Mexican on the outside, but black on the inside. She carried herself like a sister. She was a strong woman too. We were getting off to a good start, and we ended up talking for hours.

As we talked, I sensed she knew something I didn't. She kept talking about the kid issue like she slipped and said the wrong thing. I knew Charlie was hiding something from me, and everything seemed to indicate that Charlie had some other baby mommas somewhere out there.

Since we were talking about how Miss Warner's past was coming back to haunt her, I asked, "Charlie, while me and yo' mother talk about our past, would you like to join?"

Charlie frowned. "Daphne, didn't I tell you when time permits we'll talk?"

I looked at him and cut my eyes. Jessica was a woman and knew exactly what I was going through. She said, "Choo, just let it out! Right now is the best time. I mean, if Daphne really loves you, she'll understand. It will hurt, but she'll understand!"

I was blown away. I really needed to know what was going on, but Charlie was saved again! Jessica's doorbell rang. It was Jay Cooper, the family lawyer.

Charlie smiled. "Uh-oh! Looks like I'm saved by the bell. Jay Cooper is here, and we gotta go handle some business. Daphne, since my family couldn't wait 'til I handle all my business, I'll tell you what I been hiding from you later. Right now, I gotta handle some serious business and so do you, Momma, and Jessica."

Jessica went to the door to Mr. Cooper in, and he walked in looking like million dollars. I liked his style. He dressed as if he was about to attend the Academy Awards. I didn't know the designer he was wearing, but I know it cost him money. A few thousands, at least.

Charlie counted out 1.1 million to him and told Peewee and Black Dice to carry the money to his truck. After he counted all that money, it was still $2.2 million on Jessica's table.

It turned out, the money on the table was for me to open a salon, and for Jessica to open a grocery store and a few restaurants. After Charlie left with Mr. Cooper and his bodyguards, I found out that Jessica was the owner of that little Mexican restaurant I went to with Monique, Chocolate, and Mya. After I heard that, I said, "Whoa! What a small world."

I admired Jessica. She was a strong intelligent woman.

Chapter 8

Charlie

The fast life was taking its toll on me. If it wasn't one thing it was another. You'd think with the money I had, everything would be all good, but best believe, the saying, 'Mo' money, mo' problems, is true. The murder case was over, and now my problem was now Maine. He'd gotten caught in Philly with two kilos, and Bunch was dead. I received word from one of my boys in Philly, so I headed straight for West Philly from Jessica's house. Daphne was heated. I had put so much stress on her that it was taking a toll on our relationship. However, Jessica was my backbone. She and Daphne were getting along ten times better than I thought, and I was even starting to forgive my mother.

Everyone in my family was doing cool, except me. On the outside, I looked well, but I was dying on the inside. I had so much on my chest that it was killing me softly.

Jessica couldn't hold water. She had taken a liking to Daphne and she hated the fact that Daphne was in love with lies, and not me. She had put me on blast, but thanks to Jay Cooper, I was spared from a full confession. When he came to pick up Julius Henson's money and his retainer fee, it bought me a little more time to think about how I was going to explain my situation to Daphne.

She was pressed to know what I had in my closet, but I couldn't tell her while I was on the road. I promised I would tell her when I got back to Cali. It was in my best interest to do it that way. While out in Philly, I planned to see my kids, and I was hoping Maria would find it in her to let the twins come back to Cali with me for a few months.

I made it to Philly two days after Maine got cracked and Bunch was killed. I didn't know the word on Bull, but I knew either he was dead or in jail. I first got word from Gotti B, who only knew bits and pieces.

When Black Dice, Peewee, and I got to Philly, Gotti B was awaiting our arrival outside the airport. He was in a grey Range Rover with two pit bulls, Homicide and Lady. Behind him, in a 2000 Denali, were four of his soldiers.

I nodded to the four young goons before I hopped in the Range. When we hopped in, I took shotgun while Black Dice and Peewee hopped to the rear with Homicide and Lady. The two pit bulls knew Peewee and Dice, and immediately started licking their faces.

Peewee snarled, "Stop!"

Lady and Homicide were trained. They hopped behind the rear passenger seats and laid low. Gotti B took the steering wheel after he instructed his soldiers on how to trail us. He then scolded Peewee and Black dice.

"Fuck you niggaz come out here for? And Peewee you got the nerves to be hollerin' at my dogs…"

"You mean my dogs?" I cut Gotti B off.

"Yo, money, them dogs been out here with me for the last two years. I'll beat a nigga ass, messin' with my dogs."

"Aww, nigga! You ain't gonna do shit! Nigga, don't think cuz you a little younger than us, that the left coast niggaz still can't come down here and beat yo' ass. Nigga, you East Coast niggaz still learnin' about dis gangsta shit. Out West, we live by the G-code. Nigga, you better ask somebody."

As we drove off, Peewee and Gotti went on and on. They were boys. Peewee had actually taught Gotti how to use a gun. In Harlem, at age fourteen, Gotti was known on the streets as a fighter. He wasn't a gun toter until I brought Peewee and Black Dice down from the West Coast to handle Maria's brothers.

I told Gotti to stop at a corner store about two miles from the airport, and I sent him into the store to buy a newspaper. I wanted to see if Maine's arrest and Bunch's death made the paper. I was hoping it didn't, but if it did, it would give me a better understanding of what took place. Gotti only knew what got back to him in Harlem. I was going to visit Maine to get the whole run down, but I wanted to see if his story made the news or not.

As we waited for Gotti to return with the newspaper, I decided to ask Dice if he was straight. I never got the chance to apologize for shooting him, and even though it was part of the game, I hated doing it. Dice was too loyal for me not to express my deepest apologies. He was so loyal, he made it his business to fly with me and Peewee.

I wanted him to stay in Cali. I felt he needed to heal, but he said, "a gunshot wound, that ain't shit!"

After I apologized, all he did was nod. I wanted to say, "Man, you can talk, nigga! Don't start being all quiet and shit now." I didn't say anything because Dice was Dice. He was a silent assassin and true gangsta. I figured as long as he's stayin' true to the game, I should let him be.

When Gotti returned with the newspaper, I flipped through headline after headline, and didn't see anything.

"Yo, what's the deal?" Gotti asked after I closed the paper. "I got my team following us. I didn't give them any directions because I didn't know if we were hittin' the turnpike or not."

Gotti knew I wasn't about to take a chance with NYPD. They had a warrant out for me, dead or alive. They hated my young soul. Not only did I have to worry about them, I had to worry about niggas who didn't wanna see me on the streets. In my state, I was hated by many, loved by few, and respected by all.

I fixed Gotti with a look that read, 'why did you just ask that?'

He read my eyes and answered his own question. "Oh yeah! My bad. I forgot. It ain't been five straight years yet."

"No duh! Stupid," Peewee blurted.

"Yo, Peewee, shut up B," Gotti countered.

"Man, y'all don't start no East Coast-West Coast shit, a'ight."

I intervened because Peewee and Gotti were both talkative. They would have gone word for word if I let them. That's another reason I loved having Dice around. He stayed quiet and alert. He was my boy, but he was more like a professional bodyguard. Peewee, at times, talked so much I couldn't even comprehend my own thoughts.

"Look, we're not going through that turnpike. We're going to EJ's until I find out what all went down."

EJ was my brother's junior high school friend. He was a young alcoholic who got his name from the liquor E & J. My brother took care of him. When JR died, EJ took to the bottle heavy. He had no parents, and he had grown up in foster care. As a child, he stayed running away and living on the streets.

JR's death had EJ was so gone and hurt that Jessica let him have the house that he kept for JR on Chancellor Street. She knew he wasn't going to have nothing if she sold the house, and even though he was a heavy drinker, she knew he was loyal to my brother their whole friendship.

We arrived in West Philly on Chancellor Street and EJ was sitting on his porch smoking a cigarette and sipping on a fifth of his favorite liquor, E & J.

I shouted, "EJ, get yo' drunk-ass up!" as we leapt from the Range Rover.

EJ leapt up, staggered a few steps, squinted tight, looked me dead in the eyes, and shouted, "Little Charlie!"

I wasn't too pleased to see EJ so messed up that early in the day, but he was surely glad to see me. As I walked onto the porch with my whole team and two dogs, he tried to hug me. I pushed him away from me and Homicide growled.

I had mad love for EJ, but everyone knew that I hated to see my folks wasted. EJ was gone, and the smell from his Camel cigarette was giving me a headache. I told Ralph and Timbo, two of Gotti's soldiers, to carry him to the bathroom and throw him in the shower.

I was surprised when I entered the house. It was the exact same way my brother had left it. The furniture and a few other items didn't look new anymore, but they were well-kept. He had someone staying with him, judging from the way he looked outside, I knew he couldn't be keeping the house up himself. The only female I knew who would mess with EJ was Sheena.

I called into the bathroom and asked EJ who he had staying with him. Silence. No answer. A few minutes later, Timbo said, "I think he said his baby momma."

"Ask him who his baby momma?"

It took two minutes before Timbo said, "Ok, he said you should already know."

It was Sheena, which happened to be a good thing. Sheena was the only female runner my brother trusted from Philly to run for him. For some odd reason, he used to always tell me that females from L.A., Baltimore, and Philly are not to be trusted. I ended up learning the hard way in L.A. and Philly, so I chose to never test the waters in Baltimore.

Five minutes after we settled in, I got comfortable. I had lived in the house for five months when I was hopping from state to state, so this house was like home to me. I didn't know where Sheena was, because EJ was too drunk to tell me. Ralph and Timbo were having a hard time with him in the shower, so I told them to let him sleep it off.

Peewee, Gotti, Loco and Amir, Gotti's other two goons, were all on the porch smoking some green. Gotti couldn't wait to get to where we were going to post. He knew Peewee fad brought some fiyyah Cali bud. He called it Dr. Dro.

Black Dice and I were stretched out on the living room couches. We both had one leg stretched all the way out and the other on the floor. I was reading the business section of the newspaper and patting Lady on the head.

"Let me see that business section," Dice requested.

Damn, I thought. *Is dis nigga, Black Dice askin' to see the business section? Damn, my dude must know how to read stocks or sumthin'.*

I handed over the business section and asked, "Man, whachu know about the business section in the newspaper?"

Dice chuckled. "Man, a nigga only nineteen, but I know a lot about dis business shit. Especially stocks and bonds."

A snide grin spread across my face. "Fo' real?" I arched my brows in surprise..

"If I wasn't fo'real, I wouldn't be tryna read it."

"Come on, Dice! On the real, I've been knowin' you fo' almost five years, and I ain't never seen you pick up a paper. Especially not no business section."

Dice ended up knowing more than I'd thought. He sat for two hours teaching me how to read stocks. I found out that he learned from his father at age twelve how to invest. I asked, "Man, if you knew all dis a long time ago, why you just now sayin' sumthin'?"

"Shit, If I woulda known you were tryna get into stocks and bonds, like me, I woulda been said sumthin'. Shit, think about it, I work fo' you. Why wouldn't I tell you? Nigga, you got all the money, not me!"

Black Dice was right. I said, "We'll talk about dis later. I've been wanting to learn how to invest. I'm getting tired of dis street life, so make sure you remind me when we get back to Cali. I also owe you for takin' one for the team."

Sheena arrived three hours after we had settled in. When she pulled up in front of her house, she didn't know who was standing on her porch smoking.

"Sheena, damn girl! Who is all these niggaz?" Bre, Sheena's homegirl, asked.

Sheena had only left the house to take her and EJ's sons to her mother's house. By the time she got back,

I'd already invaded the castle. She started reaching in her purse.

Peewee, high as a kite, but alert, knew exactly what she was reaching for. He walked off the porch, opened the gate to the yard, and said, "Sheena, don't pull dat gun out, girl."

Sheena didn't recognize Peewee at first. The last time she'd seen him, we were fourteen. We were now eighteen. The only way she recognized him was from his L.A. Dodger fitted hat and his West Coast style. Everyone on the porch except Peewee had on Timberland boots. He had on Chuck Taylors and some Dickies.

Sheena blurted, "Oh shit! Is dat my lil' Crip homeboy, Peewee?"

"Baby, you know it's me," Peewee said in a flirtatious way. "So you didn't recognize yo' lil' Cali boyfriend, huh?"

Sheena looked past Peewee and saw me on the porch. "Charlie!" she squealed.

I was as glad to see her as she was to see me. I needed her, and I knew she needed me.

"Lil' Bruh-Bruh, how did I know you'd be out dis way?"

"Shit, you must heard about Maine and our other two Cali homeboys."

Sheena and I hugged. She kissed me on the cheek, but she reeked of Newports. I shoved her off me and backpedaled from her embrace.

"Damn, Bruh-Bruh, what I do?"

"Ma, you know I hate the smell of Newports, and you smell like a carton of them muthafuckas."

"Bruh-Bruh, do you remember when I told you I was going to stop?"

"Yep!"

"Well, I tried for about two weeks, but EJ ass done drove me back to smokin'. All he do is get on my nerves. He don't do nothing but drink, drink! JR was his only savior. Now, that he's gone, EJ is a lost cause. Matter of fact, where he at? I'm surprised he ain't on the porch smokin' and turnin' up a bottle with yo' boys."

Sheena wanted to tell me everything that was going on in Philly, but we were standing on the sidewalk in someone else's hood. I was probably supplying a few big name hustlers in Philly, but I wasn't about to stand out and be the next man's victim. Mistaken identity is a muthafucka.

I ordered everyone back into the house and sent Sheena and her girls into the kitchen. Sheena was one of the best cooks I knew. She was ten years older than me, and when I stayed in Philly, she was like my mother. She washed my clothes, made my bed, cleaned after me, and cooked up a storm every night for me.

As I sat in the living room listening to Peewee and Gotti go at it about what coast is the best, I tried to think of the best way I could go see my kids. Tracy, I knew was somewhere running around Philly, so I asked Sheena had she seen her.

Vida, one of Sheena's girls, blurted, "Oh shit! Sheena, I forgot, dat bitch is blamin' dat ugly-ass son of hers on Charlie. Charlie, you know, I'm still hotta than fish grease about dat. But baby believe me, dat baby is not yours."

I looked at Vida and cut my eyes. She was one of my ex-flings. I couldn't believe anything she said. Vida was 24 and I was 14 when I was sticking my dick in her. She wasn't pretty at all, and she ran her mouth like a faucet. I truly never understood what I saw in her.

After sleeping with Vida a few times, she singlehandedly concluded that we were a couple, and eventually she turned into a Shondella. The difference between the two was, I never impregnated Vida. It got to the point where I had to start pulling guns out on her to keep her away from me. My brother ended up banning her from the house until I moved to Cali.

"Vida, I think he asked me about Tracy, not you. He already know she's a ho' just like you, so stop hatin'. Shit, you were fuckin' him when he was only fourteen! Hell, you were rapin' the boy."

"Bitch, at least I wasn't fuckin' him and his best friend. And you know I loved him."

"Well, dat ain't none of my bizness."

Sheena and Vida started gossiping about me like I wasn't there.

I interrupted. "Damn, I didn't ask for all y'all to start gossipin'. Sheena, I need you to go find Tracy for me. I need to at least, see my son while I'm out here. Even though I don't think he's mine, I still gotta handle my bizness until I find out the truth."

"Bruh-Bruh, I already know. You don't gotta tell me. I was there when JR told you to handle yo' bizness until you get a test."

"Shit, if that's the case and it's that easy, I shoulda just came up pregnant," Vida snarled. "Shit, since, you lettin' Charlie waste money on dis bitch, I shoulda got pregnant too. Sheena, you know dat ugly lil' boy ain't his."

"If y'all don't stop talkin' and watch dat meat, y'all gon' burn something," Bre intervened from the kitchen area. She was grating cheese.

The three women were cooking tacos, but Sheena and Vida couldn't stop gossiping, and Bre was too busy flirting with Peewee. Black Dice was still slumped on the couch reading the business section of the paper and rubbing his stomach. We were starving.

"Look, we can talk later," I informed them. But, right now, y'all got nine hungry men to feed."

Bre added, "And I know who I wanna feed right now."

Peewee stopped his East Coast-West Coast feud with Gotti and said, "Who dat? Because niggaz in L.A. ain't doin' too much eatin'. We believe in getting our dick sucked and bringin' home the dough."

"Nigga stop lying'!" Bre twisted her lips. "You can make it sound good in front of yo' boys all you want, but behind closed doors you might let a bitch stick a finger in yo' ass."

The whole house filled with laughter. Even Dice had to chuckle.

Sheena added her two cents. "And that's on the real-real."

Aaahs and oooh's filled the room. The conversation had turned into sex. By the time the tacos were done, EJ had been asleep for a good five hours. Sheena went into their room and woke him up. He opened his eyes only to eat and drink a can of Pepsi, and fell back to sleep within minutes.

Talking nasty to each other had Bre feeding Peewee tacos one by one. Vida came and sat on my lap. I let her feed me a taco, but when she tried to kiss me, I shoved her off me.

"Ma, you know I'm married. Matter of fact, you gotta get off my lap."

I shoved Vida off me and walked to the back room. The house was a four bedroom. The first room EJ was in. The second and third rooms were the kids' rooms. The last room in the house was the room I called the back room. When I got to the back room, Gotti and Sheena were already in it.

Gotti was a young pussy hound. He was gaming Sheena, and she was smiling from ear to ear.

"Oh, my fault." I said and turned around.

Sheena tried to act like nothing was happening. She said, "Naw, Bruh- Bruh, it ain't even like dat. Gotti, is too young for me..."

I cut her off. "Come on, ma, I know you and yo' girls like em' young, so don't lie!"

"Yeah, ma, you know you diggin' a young nigga," added Gotti. "You just can't deny a young stud."

EJ couldn't do nothing with Sheena. He was like my father; the only thing he cared about was the bottle. I told Sheena not to feel guilty about messing with Gotti in front of me. I told her that Gotti was my young protégé, and I would love for her to be with him. Sheena was a loyal broad, especially if she had love for a nigga. She stayed ten toes down for her man.

I knew Gotti actually needed her on his team since he was now moving big weight in Harlem.

"Sheena, do you. Don't let me stop nothin'. But just know Gotti is my head man down dis way, and he's a good nigga."

I walked out of the room and spotted Peewee and Bre in the bathroom. They were fondling each other. Peewee saw me walking back toward the living room, and said, "Yo, Choo, check dis out!"

I turned around.

"Nigga, I just found the yesterday's paper on the sink. Maine is on the front page. After you read it, let me know the business, because right now a nigga bout to Crip-walk in dis pussy."

"Ha!" I couldn't help but to laugh. Peewee was in rare form.

"Plus, some mo' bitches are on the way. I had Vida and Bre call some mo' of their hoodrat ass homegirls. You know what I mean, cuuuuuzzz?"

Peewee turned into a party animal every time he hit the East Coast. I guess it was from all the attention he got. I mean, literally, females just dropped their panties once they found out he was from Cali.

"Yo, Peewee, we didn't come out here to party, homie. But since I see you already got something lined up, be ready for tomorrow."

I was exhausted. I couldn't see how Peewee could just get off a long flight then party like a rock star. For me, it was time to go to sleep. I grabbed the newspaper from Peewee and closed the bathroom door.

The rest of Sheena's pussy pound had arrived. I knew most of them because they all got around. Out of the five that had arrived, I'd fucked four of them. They were all at least five years older than everyone in my crew. The youngest broad in their circle was Bre. She was 24. The oldest nigga in my crew was Dice. He'd just turned nineteen.

As I walked into the living room, Diamond, one of the broads who had robbed me for some of my youth, was asking Dice about the West Coast. He wasn't paying her any mind. He was fighting sleep. We were both tired. He had the newspaper covering the tech-nine on his lap and his hand covering his face. He was dozing off and didn't want anyone to know.

The local hoodrats greeted me with their flirtatious, hellos trying to throw me the pussy. Vida sensed what each of them was trying to do, and said, "Y'all, guess what?"

"What, bitch?" Judy asked. Judy was the only one out of the five that I hadn't fucked. All of Sheena's homegirls were pretty, except Vida, so best believe I tried to fuck Judy on numerous occasions. Judy had a big booty. We called her Big Booty Judy.

Judy never gave me any attention. I figured either my brother was sticking his dick in her, or she wasn't feeling me. I never came to understand why, but she knew I was a beast in the bed because I'd fucked her whole crew.

"Charlie done got married on all of us!"

I shook my head and tapped Dice on the shoulder. He groaned "Aww cuzz, dat shit hurt!"

I had forgotten about Dice's shoulder, so I apologized. I felt bad. Guilty. I cursed myself, "Damn!" I was supposed to have known better.

"Come on, homie, let's go lay it out in the kid's room. But, once again, I didn't mean to do dat."

Dice hopped up, tucked his tech-nine at waist level, and walked to EJ's son's room. The room had two twin beds in it. Ralph followed Dice and I into the room along with Homicide and Lady.

"Yo, homie, what's the deal?" he asked. "Can we post up with these hoes or what?"

Ralph was Gotti's right hand man. He knew that since we were locking ourselves in the room, he had to run the living room. I laughed inwardly, and settled in one of the twin-sized beds. Sheena and Gotti were in the back room, and she was moaning at the top of her lungs.

Dats my young nigga, I thought. *Nigga, I hope you have a jimmy hat on. Cuz bitches are scandalous. They'll put a baby on you real fast.*

My heart nearly stopped when I opened the newspaper and saw Maine's mug shot. The headline over his picture read,

3 Dead, 2 in jail after Federal Raid...

"Damn," I said when I read the headline. I looked over at Dice to show him, but he was sleep.

I read the rest of the article.

> *Eighteen-year-old Maine Jacob of Queens, New York, and Eighteen-year-old Justin Turner of Los Angeles, California, were arrested today on charges that range from triple homicide to drug trafficking. Yesterday, federal agents, who have been watching and waiting six months for Maine Jacob to return to Philadelphia, were caught in a drug raid gone bad. Two agents were killed, along with another suspect from Jacob's organization. Turner, another member of Jacob's enterprise, is currently in critical condition.*
>
> *Jacob is being held without bond, and Turner is in federal custody while he clings to life at Mercy-Fitzgerald Hospital.*

The article didn't say much, but at least I got an insight on what took place. I closed the newspaper and set it on the floor next to Lady. I stretched out on the bed, and I guess that was the key Homicide and Lady were waiting for. They hopped on the bed and lay next to me. There wasn't enough room for all of us, so I ordered them back on the floor.

I loved my dogs. I'd raised them from puppies, rained them, and I had slept with them many nights. But it wasn't enough room for all of us, so they had to be mad.

As soon as I started dozing off, Vida knocked on the room door. I was going to ignore her, but my dogs started pacing the room back and forth in circles.

I shouted, "Yo. Go away! Niggas tryna sleep!"

Vida smacked her lips and walked off. I was proud of myself. For the first time in my life, I had turned down some pussy. I started thinking about Daphne and how I was changing for her.

Before I went to sleep, I said a quick prayer. "God, I know I can be a one woman man. Please, just guide me through the motions."

Chapter 9

Daphne

After seven months of being with Charlie, I was head-over hills in love with him. However, my woman's intuition was right! I thought I was just being insecure, but after Charlie went to Philadelphia, everything was revealed to me. He was just like my father, a goddamn rolling stone. It seemed that ever since Jessica put him on blast about asking me to marry him, but not cleaning out his closet, everything has fallen apart.

It didn't take long to find out that he had another baby momma out in the world. I somewhat knew it, but I was in denial. When I found out, it felt like someone had stuck a dagger in my heart. I had stayed at Jessica's house for two days straight after Charlie went out of state. Jessica and I were working together to get my beauty salon started. On the second day, she asked me to stay at her house because she was waiting for an important call. She was waiting on the city to call her back about a vacant lot she wanted to purchase.

After she left, I sat in the house watching BET's 106 & Park. Ms. Warner and Jessica's kids were gone shopping. I had the house to myself, but I stayed posted in the living room by the phone.

It was 10:30 in the morning, and an hour after Jessica left, the phone rang. I figured it to be the city, so I answered professionally.

"You have reached the Warner residence."

To my surprise, a female asked, "May I speak to Jessica?"

"She's not in. Wanna leave a message?"

"Yes. Can you tell her that Charlene, Charlie's baby momma, called?"

My heart skipped a beat, dropped to my stomach, then jumped back up to my chest. I thought I was having a heart attack. I couldn't believe my ears. I was so shocked, I repeated baby momma twice.

"Yes. Charlie's baby momma."

Charlene was cool, calm and collected. She said, 'Yes. Charlie's baby momma,' like it wasn't nothing. "My name is Charlene. I'm not callin' to start any baby momma drama. I'm just callin' to talk to Jessica about Charlie's daughter."

Charlene was about to hang up, but I needed to know more. I said, "Hol' on. Don't hang up. I see you ain't acting like most baby mommas, so if you don't mind, can I please ask you a few questions?"

"As long as you make sure Charlie keeps his responsibilities, I don't mind."

"That's a deal!"

"Well, what may I help you with?"

"Well, first, I wanna know what state are you in? And how old is your daughter by Charlie?"

"Charlena is four months old, and I'm in Atlanta, Georgia."

I thought, *no wonder she's so polite. She's a southern belle.*

"How old are you?"

"I'm 21."

"How did you and Charlie meet?"

"It's a long story, but we met at Cascades. Cascades is a skating rink out here in Atlanta. We were a couple until he cheated on me with a stripper."

"So he cheated on you with a stripper?"

"Damn!" I blurted. The phone started to click. The city was on the other line. I told Charlene I had to go and clicked over.

"Hello!"

"Hi! Is Jessica Warner in?"

"No she's not. May I take a message?"

"Yes. Can you tell her to call David Peters at City Hall? She can call me between now and five o' clock."

I agreed to deliver the message and hung up.

Jessica returned around 3pm. About this time, I was ready to go. I'd been crying for about five hours. Charlie lied to me. I was played. My mother told me! I should have listened. Jessica knew he had another baby momma. I started wondering if she was ever going to tell me that Charlie was nothing but lies. She was his sister, and she kept telling me she wanted to see us get married. She acted like she liked me. She was a woman, so I figured she'd at least say, *Daphne, Charlie really loves you, but he's no good.*

However, truthfully speaking, she wasn't at fault. I just had to blame someone other than myself for my heartache. And the person that I needed to blame was out of state.

Jessica knew I was depressed as soon as she entered the house. "Daphne, what's wrong with you? Girl, it looks like you've been crying all morning."

I wanted to say, *Bitch, I have! And you know what's wrong with me.* But, I said, "I'm hurting. Yo' brotha got me fucked up. He played me!"

"What happened, girl? He's home already?"

"No. His baby momma called here and told me to tell you she called."

"Who?"

"His baby momma!"

Jessica acted as if she didn't know who I was talking about. *Bitch, don't act like you don't know.* I screamed inside. However, I kept my smart comment to myself.

"Oh, his baby momma!" she said with a puzzled look. I was starting to think it was more than one. Eventually, I would find this to be true.

"Oh, where she say she's at?"

Damn, do dis bitch s'pose to be comin' out here? Why is she askin' where she at? Is she tryna figure out what baby momma I'm talkin' bout? Shit, I shoulda asked Charlene if she knew of any other baby mommas Charlie might have that I should know about. Man, dis nigga Charlie is just like my no good ass father. I can't believe I'm in love with a hoe!

"Daphne, I asked where she's at?"

I was hotter than fish grease and frustrated. Jessica was starting to irritate me. I yelled "Why?"

She countered, "Girl, don't start yellin'!"

I couldn't take it. I forgot she was his sister, not mine. The best thing I could do at the moment was leave.

I said, "You know what, Jessica, I don't know why I even answered yo' fuckin' phone for you, but I did. And the best thing to do now is to leave. So tell yo' lyin'-ass brotha don't call me, and I'm going back home."

I got up from the couch and wobbled my big self over to grab my car keys. When I grabbed them, Jessica said, "Daphne, I know, you might be mad at me too, but you know I couldn't tell you. Please, don't be mad at me. I know how you feel, and I've told Charlie about this. Daph, you do not have to leave. It's not good to stress while you're pregnant. Just stay here with me."

I felt so played. All I could say was, "I can't!"

I made it home about 6pm. I had left Jessica's around 3:50. From the San Gabriel Valley to Hawthorne, California is an hour drive at the most, but it took me two hours. I drove like I was driving Miss Daisy while contemplating my next move. I debated with myself the whole drive if I should go back to my father's house, the projects, or home. I took my time contemplating. When I finally came to a decision, I decided to sit it out and wait to hear what Charlie had to say. I was far too gone to just up and leave. My love for Charlie wasn't that easy; it wouldn't let me leave.

As I leapt from my car, Chocolate, Mo'nique, Joyce, and Mya were walking out of the apartment complex gate. I looked at Mya and tried to hide the dried up tears at the corner of my eyes and the depression on my face. I didn't need her to know that Charlie was just like my father, because she would have been trying to get me to go back home. Mya was my true best friend out of her and Monique.

Chocolate, Joyce, and Monique were all as big as I was, but Chocolate and I were the biggest. We were roughly the same size. Looking at them, I felt cold and hot. I felt good knowing that I wasn't the only one pregnant, but also felt bad because I knew I was pregnant by a man who I really didn't know. My dreams were becoming a nightmare.

As I walked to the apartment security gate, Mya asked me, "Girl, where have you been for the last few days?"

"Gone," I replied.

"Slut, I know dat. But I asked where have you been?"

Mya didn't know I was heated, so I shifted my weight from one leg to the next and put my hands on my hips. I was trying to hide my emotions, but Mo'nique hissed,

"Shit, sho' look like somebody ain't been havin' a good day."

Chocolate and Joyce chimed in. "Uh-huh!"

I was starting not to like them. It was something about them that was fake. I meant to ask Ms. Warner about them, but when Charlie called, my mind flipped. She never mentioned them in her life story about how she became sprung. The only daughter she talked about was Jessica, her daughter-in-law.

I cut my eyes at them and asked, "Uh-huh what? Watchu hoes uh-huh'n fo'?"

"Girl, it looks like Charie done made you mad. I mean, if it ain't him, somebody got under yo' skin."

Chocolate was prying. She was trying to pick my brain to see what was wrong with me. I ignored her.

"Anyway, where y'all going?"

"To the Laugh Factory," Mya said. "Joyce done came up with some tickets."

I replied, "Oh, okay! I don't wanna hold y'all up, so I'm 'bout to go in dis house."

"Girl, I got an extra ticket if you wanna come."

Chocolate immediately shifted her weight off her right leg and pouted. I wanted to say, *Bitch, is there a problem?* A lot of jealousy had been displayed in the last few months between us, but I couldn't understand why. Charlie was her brother, but I was his fiancé. I was really starting to sense it was more to the picture.

Shit, the way this bitch actin', Charlie might have lied about dis bitch being his sister. She sho' is startin' to act like there's a problem between us. Shit, the bitch might be fuckin' her own brother.

Joyce knocked me out of my thoughts. "Girl, I said, I got another ticket. Do you wanna come?"

I really didn't want to go to the Laugh Factory, but since Chocolate was acting as if she had a problem with me going, I said, "Yeah, I'll go, but first, I gotta go wash up."

While I went to wash up, Chocolate, Joyce, and Mo'nique went to KFC. Mya stayed with me. She knew something was bothering me, but didn't ask what's wrong. I guess she knew I didn't want to talk about it.

As I stood in the shower washing my ass, she stood at the entrance of the bathroom talking.

"Daph, you know Mo'nique's baby daddy is in jail?"

"Yep." I replied. "How you know?"

"He called her dis morning from Philadelphia. I told her not to mess with his ass. Now her baby gotta grow up without a father. She says he left her some money, but I don't think so. That's why I'm waitin' to get outta college before I have any kids. I gotta be ready."

"Mya, you're not Miss Goody Too Shoes, so stop actin' innocent," I said while washing between my legs and thinking about Charlie's lying ass.

Mya stood at the bathroom entrance the whole time I got ready for the Laugh Factory. She was my girl, so I didn't feel like my privacy was being violated. But as I dried off, she said, "Damn, girl, yo titties done got supa big!"

I looked at my best friend and frowned. "Mya, I'm glad you see I'm getting big as a house, but girl do not be lookin' at me like dat. Shit, I'm startin' to wonder about you. You don't have a man, you stay male bashin', and I can't tell if you're gay or not, but do not look at me like dat!"

To my surprise, Mya replied, "Daph, if I was gay, I've already eyefucked you, so don't worry!"

I could've snapped. I didn't know how to respond. Was Mya gay, or was she just playing with me? I wasn't sure what she was, but one thing was fo' sho', I wasn't trying to find out. I changed the subject.

The Laugh Factory was crowded when I pulled into the parking lot behind Chocolate. I had decided to drive my car, since I couldn't ride with Chocolate because I felt she was as fake as a three dollar bill. There was something within me telling me to keep her close, yet far. I went with my first mind, so Mya and I rode in my Lexus.

Mo'nique surprised me when she didn't want to ride with us. I figured it was because she didn't want to hear Mya talk about what we should and shouldn't be doing. But even though Mya was good at telling someone what they should and shouldn't be doing, I knew that wasn't the reason Mo'nique didn't want to ride with us. Mo'nique was starting to act fishy too.

Joyce, out of the three, was unpredictable. One day she'd be cool and easy to get along with, then the next day she'd act snobbish. My intuition told me she was not to be trusted. I felt as if I was caught up in a world of drama. I mean, every which way I turned, it was some kind of problem. I don't know if I was trippin' or not, but I knew something wasn't right.

When we parked, Joyce handed everyone their tickets. She said, "These tickets are courtesy of some nigga named Mario. So y'all say thanks Mario."

"Thanks, Mario," we said in unison.

Inside the comedy club, we situated ourselves at one of the tables in front of the stage. Before we sat down, I gave Mya a fifty-dollar bill and told her to go buy us some buffalo wings. I didn't offer anyone else at our table anything. I treated them with the same courtesy Mya and I received when the three bad wolves came back from KFC. They offered us nothing; not even a bone.

While Mya was ordering our food, some nigga who resembled Chris Rock came on stage. He was the master of ceremony. I forgot his name, but he immediately attacked our table. I guess that was to be expected with four pregnant girls sitting right by stage.

He started his set by asking the crowd, "How's everybody doin'?"

The crowd replied, "Fine!"

"Well, I'm glad to see so many black folks in the house tanite!"

"Sheeeit, we even got a few Caucasians, betta known as crackas, in the houuuuuuse!" The MC paused, gazed into the audience, and shouted, "Daaaaayum!"

The club filled with laughter, figuring he was about to say something hilarious.

"Y'all, we even got a few chow mein rice in here. Look at 'em! Whacha'll names? Kim Lee and Chebang Chung or sumthin'? I wanna thank y'all fo' comin' out, but I know from living in the hood, all y'all want me to do is hurry up and buy. So I'll hurry up and buy y'all attention in just a minute."

At that moment, Mya returned with the Buffalo wings. The MC spotted us as she sat down, and he did a Martin on us.

"Awww dayuuuuuuuum, Geeeeeena! Damn! Damn! Damn! Damn! We even got the goddam Baby Momma Drama Committee in the houuuuuuse!"

He was so funny. I laughed so hard my stomach started to hurt.

"Okay, y'all, befo' I introduce the first comedian onto stage, let me say dis to the BMDC... Don't start no shit..."

The MC pointed the mic our way and the crowd yelled, "WON'T BE NO SHIT!"

After the MC did his thing, he introduced the first act. The comic called herself Blackalious. I immediately didn't like her. Her act made Chocolate feel like she was the shit. Blackalious started off by saying, "I'm a proud dark skin woman! And I want all dark skin bitches to be proud too! See, I was one of them sistas that them light skin heifers always picked on. They called me names like Tar Baby, Darth Vador, and Spot. See, ever since I was ten, I've always hated light skin bitches. I'm soo serious about pushing dis darkness. I get into it with whoever ain't representin' dis darkness like me..."

Chocolate chimed in. "I know that's right, girl." She looked at me and rolled her eyes.

I just shook my head. *Oh no dis bitch didn't!* I didn't say a word. I kept to myself and waved Chocolate off. She was a hater. I didn't have time to sit up and listen to Blackalious stroke Chocolate's ego, so I grabbed my shit and told Mya, "I'm boutta go. You stayin' or goin'?"

Mya picked up our buffalo wings and said, "Girl, you know I'm leavin' with you."

I looked over at Mo'nique like, 'are you coming or what?' She didn't say a word, so Mya and I left. I just couldn't wait to finally question Charlie about his funny acting ass relatives. Something just wasn't right about these hoes, and I sick and tired of the bullshit.

Chapter 10

Charlie

I woke up the next morning tired after Vida kept me up all night. She tried on ten different occasions to get in the room, but she was unsuccessful. I stuck to my guns and fought the temptation. Black Dice was so tired he slept through everything. It surprised me because he wasn't a hard sleeper. I guess he felt protected with Lady and Homicide in the room.

When I got up, I had to wake everyone in the house up. I was glad EJ was still in his drunk-coma, because it would have been some shit. In the back room, Gotti and Sheena were asleep on top of the covers, ass naked. I knew Sheena wasn't messing with EJ on a relationship level, but it was the principle that she was EJ's baby momma, and fucking Gotti in his house.

Gotti would have beat EJ half to death if anything would have gone wrong, but I was glad it didn't. I already had a lot of bullshit on my hands. I woke Gotti up and slapped Sheena on the ass.

She groaned, "Aaah!" as she woke up. "Damn, Bruh-Bruh, you didn't have to do that."

"Shut up, ma," Gotti said. "If you woulda locked the do' like I told you, you wouldn't be havin' no rude awakenings..."

I cut Gotti off. "Look, I don't care about all dat bullshit. Nigga, don't neva let a bitch decide how you secure yourself while getting some pussy. Anyhow, Sheena, you know dis shit ain't cool. You wanted EJ to catch y'all because you tired of his ass. I should be flippin' the script on yo' ass, but don't pull dis janky ass shit again!"

"Bruh-Bruh, you know it ain't like dat. EJ knows we ain't together no more. I can fuck whoever I wanna fuck. Dat nigga do him, I do me."

Sheena didn't realize how trifling that looked on her end. She figured just because she wasn't sleeping with EJ, she could just sleep with another man in his house. That was not the business. However, I couldn't talk. I was sleeping with my fiancé's best friend, so who was I?

I decided to change the subject. Shit, if you asked me, it was a dog eat dog world.

"Anyhow, fuck the bullshit. Gotti, go wake up yo' crew. I need y'all to hit the turnpike. Go to the city and pick up my twins. If Maria don't wanna let them come without her, bring her too. I gotta see my kids! And when you pick them up, make sure it's safe to roll out with my kids. I want top security on my kids, dawg. Also, tell Ralph to stay put. I like him. He gon' roll with me today. Plus, you gon' need room in dat Range Rover for my kids and Maria. Didn't you tell me both vehicles were bulletproof?"

Gotti nodded. "Yep."

"Well, that's good."

"Sheena, you go get yo' posse up. Tell 'em to go get dressed. Send 'em to the mall to get us some clothes. I need you to go find Tracy too. Tell her I will be in town tomorrow, and I need a number to contact her. Do not tell her I'm already out here. Today, Maria might be here, so I don't need no shit. Also, before EJ get up, go buy him a few fifths. Put them by his bed. I need to keep him outta the way for now."

I handed Sheena a wad of money, $5,000. She hopped up and got straight to business.

I went back to the room Dice and I had slept in, and Peewee was in the room bragging about his rendezvous with Bre.

"Yeah, cuzz, the bitch gives some bomb ass head. She was tryna turn a young nigga out. I mean, the pussy is a'ight, but on Crip, the bitch let me hit dat ass too…"

I shook my head and cut Peewee off. "A'ight, Mr. Marcus, you could brag about yo' affair later. As of now, we gotta go see Maine and Bull."

Peewee countered, "Yeah nigga, we already knew dat. But I rather be Mr. Marcus with a condom than Bare Back King with ten baby mommas and 100 maybes."

That was a low blow. I was about to counter, but Ralph entered the room. "Charlie, I heard you and the two big homies from Cali are lettin' the kid roll with y'all."

I cracked a one-sided smile. "Yeah, it's yo' lucky day."

I liked Ralph. He was only sixteen, but he had a lot of pride about himself. He was a respectable young nigga. He, Gotti, and their crew were raised Muslims. I liked their beliefs, so I took them under my wing. In comparison to Gotti, I liked Ralph most. He reminded me of my brother. He was a real leader because he stayed asking what he didn't know, and stayed thinking before he'd act. I couldn't knock Gotti as their commander in chief, because Gotti was just like me. Stupid, dumb, smart, all rolled in one. His stupid-ass went in Sheena raw dog! Ralph was smart enough to protect himself. He reminded me of my brother so much. He was a young general waiting to happen.

After everyone washed up and ate breakfast, we teamed up and went our separate ways. As my team walked out the door, I looked at Ralph and told him, "Man, you remind me so much of my brother."

He replied, "I take that as a good thang."

Homicide barked with his head moving up and down. It was as if he knew what we were talking about.

"See, even my dog agree with dat."

My brother's death marked the start of a nightmare for me. All the women I played were coming back to haunt me, I had to shoot one of my own comrades, and my best friend was behind bars facing life. It wasn't until I visited Maine in a federal jail that I realized all of my nightmares were becoming reality.

I never thought I would see my best friend behind bars. I thought Maine and I were untouchable. We were the kings of the East Coast and West Coast drug trade. We were one of a kind, and above the law. Well, that's what I thought...

When Ralph and I checked into the federal lockup facility to see Maine, I almost cried. We had to go through so many gates and doors; I lost count before we got to the visiting area. Then, when we made it to the visiting area, we had to wait more than an hour just to see him.

As we waited, I thought about Black Dice and Peewee. I'd sent them on the other side of the institution to see Bull. Bull was in the medical module. He was now in stable condition and had been moved to the jail right before we arrived. I was hoping Dice and Peewee didn't have to go through the same hassle Ralph and I were going through. With Peewee's temper, I didn't need them to go through any hassles.

When Maine walked into the visiting area, I felt tears rush my eyes. I'd already told myself that this was not the place I wanted to see my best friend, but as he took his seat, the flood gates broke. Maine looked a hot mess. He had spotted eyes, his nose was crooked, and his top lip had a 3-inch gash.

"Yo, before you ask what happened, let me say three things," he said. "Choo, I fucked up. You were right and I didn't listen."

I wanted to say, *No muthafuckin' duh!* I'd told Maine all along to stop playing with the Feds. I was kinda mad at him because he didn't listen and we'd lost some valuable comrades over his stupidity and his hardheadedness. That was not fair to me, and I wanted to beat Maine over the head for his careless actions. However, I didn't want to add fuel to the fire, so I just said, "Man, a hard head makes a soft ass."

Ralph chimed in. "That's some real shit."

Maine glanced at Ralph and snarled, "Mind yours, youngsta. Also, dis spot not the spot, so as Peewee would say, cuzz, gangsta move up outta dis joint with no hesitation as soon as the kid tie them boots. Yaaaada?"

I shook my head. Ralph looked as if he didn't understand anything that Maine had said. I was glad he didn't. That meant the Feds probably wouldn't know the twisted West Coast lingo either. I admit, I was even fascinated with the way Peewee and many other Crips had their own lingo. It was unique.

"So they got the locsta on er' thin'. Dat kid B.B. King can keep it movin' on some straight forward type shit. Dem Luv Puttins iz hotta than fish grease. Yaaaada?"

I shook my head in agreement once more. Maine was telling me to go legit and get out the game. The feds had put everything on him. He was giving me the heads up that our empire had crumbled.

"Now, on da thang-thang, Bitch Boy outta RA went shank. Cuzz had Luv Puttins campaignin'. When G-sta and the hands made it to the pentagon, Bitch Boy had Luv Puttin on board. Luv Puttin kick da deeez-zay. On #1, got off as soon as Mighty Mouse tried to come save the deez-zay. Loco, da sheeeeit was like red and blue. H-O #2, knocked G-sta to the greezy and murked the Bitch Boy worker. Then, cuzz, gangsta moved on a Puttin. Cuzz, get an A+, but Puttin hit cuzz more times than once. The kid faded out on the spot. G-sta seen dat and flipped his wig. H-O #1 seen da same thang and ran to cover his boy, but Puttin hit him with three to the chest. G-sta grabbed cuzz and stayed low until Puttin did their thang."

I sat shaking my head nonstop. Tears rushed my eyes and down my cheeks in rivers. I cursed myself. Maine told me everything that the newspaper said, but I had to find out who was the snitch. I also wanted to know what happened to his face. I needed to know who was responsible. I had the money and connections to place a hit with the quickness on whoever was responsible. I looked at Maine and asked, "Man, what's the biz on Bitch Boy? And what happened to the G-sta?"

Maine just shook his head.

"Man, da G-sta is all fucked up. Luv Puttin, put major hands and feet on the kid. After G-sta and H-O #1 laid low and after Luv Puttin stopped spittin' shells, they beat the kid like a runaway slave. They even tried to smash H-O #1 while he was already hit, so G-sta got up and rushed the whole pack. G-sta said he think er' thin' on his body is broke…"

I cut Maine off. "Damn, my nig…" I paused. I hated seeing my boy like this. "But don't trip, tell G-sta Jay Cooper is already on the case. He's puttin' a team of lawyers together as we talk. B.B. King will call him as soon as he gets a chance. He s'pose ta tell Jay that G-sta need some medical treatment and the people ain't tryna give him none."

Maine nodded an agreement.

"Cuzz, Bitch Boy straight renegading out there."

Bout time, nigga, I thought. That's all I needed to know. I waved Maine off. I didn't need to hear no more about his case. After I told him I got everything under control, he hopped out of his visiting chair and said, "Choo, I'm up shit's creek, homie. I trust you as my best friend and as my brotha, so I know you will take care of Nikki and my two sons. She got some dough put up for days like dis, but you know the biz, that shit only gon' last so long. Also, dat bitch Mo'nique keep tellin' me dat dat baby is mine, but it could be any of ours, so get a test. B, I want a test as soon as possible. However, I'm askin' you as my nigga to add my two and a half to yo' twenty, and treat them like yours."

"You got dat," I assured Maine as we stood to hug.

After our brotherly hug, Maine looked at Ralph and said, "Ock, you see where I'm headed, so make sure you keep yo' head above water and stay sucka free, because if you don't, you gon' drown. And drownin' up in dis river is not the way to go out. You under—"

I had to cut Maine off. The whole visit he was talking like he had already received 500 years.

"Maine, you need to stop talkin' like there's no light at the end of tunnel."

"Nigga, it ain't!" Maine countered. "Shit, matter of fact, go to the stash, grab my cut, shoot it to Jessica, and tell her to open up a few restaurants down in Miami. Tell her that she and Nikki can co-own them. Fuck usin' any of my money on Jay Cooper and his law firm. Choo, I'm a thug. I know when I had it good, and I know when I'm going to have it bad. It's no way outta dis, so a nigga gotta ride dis one out. So if the feds is listenin' to dis conversation, they got the leader of the empire they've been tryin' to catch."

I hated Maine's statement. He had only been down for a few days and was already talking crazy. Ralph and I hurried up and got out of that federal facility. I felt bad. My empire was crumbling right before my eyes, and it was as if God wouldn't stop letting my life go downhill.

When we got to the Denali, Black Dice and Peewee were still visiting Bull. As we waited inside the truck, Homicide and Lady laid low in the rear. I guess they were tired from sitting in the truck all day and staying up all night. I ended up explaining my situation to Ralph. I told him to never get caught up like I did. I told him to find a righteous woman and stick it out with her.

"Ralph, life is hectic on these streets. You and Gotti is makin' money now. They say money, power, respect is what the game consists of, but that's not all. To get money, you gotta have some power and respect. To get power and respect, you gotta set a few examples. A few examples can come from anything that's gon' get you notoriety. Notoriety in the streets consist of anything outrageous and out of the ordinary. Meaning, you gotta do something terrifying that's gonna make people remember. Once they remember, they either gon try to eat with you or ride against you. The ones who decide to eat with you feel what you do, or just wanna move with a new team, but the ones who decide to ride against you look at you as a threat and need to find a way to get you outta their way. Dis can be either through war, snitchin', or just plain out strategizing you.

"Now, after all dis take place, you get the groupies. It's like you become an overnight celebrity. Females gon' be throwin' you the pussy left to right. You become a dolla sign to them. That's why all these rappers, actors, athletes and all these other famous muthafuckas keep going through it with these different women. If it ain't baby momma drama, it's a lawsuit for rape or some mo' bullshit. The only reason all dis shit be takin' place is because of money.

"See, dis is the side the homies in the hood ain't tellin' you young niggas. They ain't tellin' a nigga about the humiliation, the troubles, the heartaches, the pain, and all the penitentiary chances one will have to take. They ain't tellin' niggas about the strain a nigga family goes through, all the children who will be brought into dis world fatherless or motherless. Shit, all in all, karma is a muthafucka. Everything you do or did to get yo' money, power, respect is gon' come back and haunt you, especially if you ain't getting' yo' money in a positive way. Ralph, what I'm getting at is, you and Gotti got money, power and respect, now y'all gotta worry about the groupies and the haters. I know I sound like a hypocrite because I didn't practice what I'm preaching, but dis is my life experience. My brother tried to warn me, but I was hard headed. I just hope you take heed to what I'm sayin', because you see I may never see my best friend out on the streets with me again. Dis street life is a mutha—"

"Cuzz, unlock da do'."

I was cut off in mid-sentence by Peewee. I'd been so deep in conversation with Ralph, I didn't see Peewee and Black Dice approaching the truck. I was slippin', and knew I was going to get an ear full from my head henchman.

I hit the unlock button and Peewe went in. "Cuzz, you can't be slippin' like dat, Choo. Nigga, we coulda had yo' head."

I stayed quiet, knowing I was in for a long drive. By the time we made it onto EJ's block, I'd gotten a full lecture on my suicidal mistake. Dice stayed quiet like always. The only voice heard the whole ride was Peewee's.

He told me that Bull told him the same thing Maine told me. Bull was wounded badly. I told him the police beat Maine like a runaway slave. Our conversation ended when we parked and Peewee vowed to kill Fat Rat. Fat Rat was the Fed's informant that we nicknamed Bitch Boy. Peewee had given him that name after he bitch slapped him for stepping on his white gators and not excusing himself.

As we hopped out the Denali, I nodded my head, approving the next mission at hand.

Peewee cracked a devilish grin. "Well, give me the keys." I handed him the keys to the truck and he got right to work giving orders.

"Ralph, go in dat house and tell one of them hoes to find you a screwdriver, and tell Latif and Amir to watch Charlie step by step, because he's a lil' discombobulated about Maine. After you do dat, we out. Bouta teach you how us L.A. niggaz get down."

I got a call from Gotti B about thirty minutes after Peewee, Black Dice, and Ralph left on their mission. I was sitting in the house talking to Sheena about Tracy. Tracy had told Sheena that she didn't have a phone for me to call her on, but she would come see me to let me know how to get in contact with her. My phone rang at that very moment.

When I answered, Gotti said, "Yo, I'm at Maria's crib. I got the kids, but she wanna talk to you."

I knew Maria was going to send me through hell and back to let Gotti bring my kids to see me. I looked at Sheena and the rest of her clique and walked to the back room. When I entered the room, I told Gotti to put Maria on the phone.

"Charlie, we really need to talk. I don't mind you takin' the kids, but I need to talk to you."

As Maria spoke, I immediately sensed something was wrong. I asked, "Maria, what's wrong?"

"Charlie, I can't tell you over the phone, but I need help!"

Maria started sobbing. I didn't know what could have been wrong, but I felt she needed me by her side. I immediately told her to pass Gotti back the phone.

"Aiyo, what's wrong with shawty?"

"That's what I'm tryna find out. Shawty just started boo-hoo'n for nothin'."

"A'ight. Ock, get 'em here as fast as possible, but handle my kids with care."

"Aiyo, Ock, I been helpin' you raise these kids since day one, so I don't need all the extra handle with care bullshit, a'ight? A nigga will take a bullet to the head before I let anything happen to our angels. Nah mean?"

I agreed. Gotti was right. I was being overprotective for no good reason. Gotti played father to the twins on a daily basis. He was the one who took them shopping on my behalf. He was the one who helped give them their first, second, third, and fourth birthday parties. He was the one who picked them up on weekends and took them out to theme parks. Actually, he was the one performing all of my fatherly duties for me.

I hung up with Gotti after he said they'd be on their way after he stopped to get Maria and the kids something to eat. I closed my phone and got ready to walk back into the living room, but my phone went off again soon as I entered.

"Yo."

"Yo, my ass!" It was Jessica. "Charlie, you need to get back down here as soon as possible! Daphne is mad as hell at you. She knows about Charlene..."

"Damn! Jess, how did she find out about Charlene? Ma, I pray to gawd dat you didn't tell her my business."

"No, crazy!" Jessica snapped. "I was gone to get the papers for that vacant lot, the one we gon' use to open up our shopping center. That's when Charlene called. She was callin' because she wanna take the test to prove that you are the father of her daughter. Daphne was the only one home when she called, and Charlene told her everything about you and her."

"Damn!" I said again.

"Jess, where's she at now? Let me talk to her."

"Choo, that girl stormed outta dis house like a bat outta hell. Shit, she was so mad, she was ready to beat my ass. She told me to tell you she going back to her father's house and don't call!"

My heart skipped a beat. I had to count 1-2-3 and breathe. I was discombobulated. I'd dealt with issues ten times worse than this, but this was the first time I'd ever felt my heart literally being pulled out of my chest.

I was hurt for a few seconds then I realized I had to pull myself together. I told Jessica that Maria was bringing the twins to come see me, so I'll talk to her later. I hung up, shook my head in disbelief, and walked back into the living room. My life was taking hit after hit. When it rained, it poured!

In the living room, Sheena and her crew were gossiping about everything and everybody in Philly. It was as if they all were giving a testimonial. All I heard was,

"Uh-huh." "Yeah." "I know that's right." "Girl, he said..." "Girl, she said..." "No he didn't." "Guuuuurrrl."

The dick hounds were something else. I just shook my head. I hated that they sat for hours talking about nothing. I guess I hated that quality about all females, because from state to state, coast to coast, women had one thing in common; they gossiped. If it wasn't a beauty salon, it was at one of their girlfriend's house. I never understood why broads gossiped about everything under the sun.

It was 12:30pm and I was already exhausted from my day. And to make things worse, I came to a house filled with ghettofied-drama queens. I looked at everyone in attendance and frowned. Latif and Amir stood at the front entrance pestering EJ. He was on the porch drunk. He'd only been awake for about three hours, and was gone already. I felt bad for him, but thought, fuck 'em! He's just like my bottle head old man.

Sheena, Vida and the rest of their clique were all staring at me. I guess, they were all wondering what I was thinking. I had a disgusted look on my face and they knew I wasn't feeling the environment. I looked at the clouds of tobacco and weed smoke that filled the air and thought of my kids.

"Aiyo!" I yelled. "Man, y'all turn off dat loud ass music and open up some of these windows. Y'all, givin' a nigga a headache. Y'all, got the music sky high, but y'all steady talkin' over it! Y'all smokin' them goddamn cancer sticks and don't even care dat two lil' ones be runnin' around dis joint. Matter fact, party is over! Dis shit ain't even cool, especially when I'm in town. I got my baby momma and my kids on the way, so y'all gots ta go. If you don't live here, bounce!"

Big Booty Judy frowned. "Damn, Charlie, you come all the way from Cali on some otha shit. A bitch knows ya boy made headlines, but don't take it out on us. Nigga, we done went shoppin' fo' you and yo' team, and dis how you treat us? You come in the house, don't speak, yo' phone ring, you walk to the back room, then you come back in here and trip on us. Didn't JR tell you that the bitch is the deadly piece in the game of life?"

I was cornered. The walls were closing in on me and the streets were taking it's toll. *Judy is right,* I thought. *These hoes ain't been nothing but loyal to me. Even though I don't trust any one of these bitches, I know they got my back.*

I snapped out of my thoughts and said, "Judy, you right. A nigga is trippin', but it ain't like what you think. I'm not sayin' fuck y'all. I'm just sayin' get out! My kids bout ta be in dis house right now, and it's not cool for y'all to just be sitting around smokin' dat stanky-ass shit in here. It smells like hot ass, pussy, cigarettes, weed, roach spray, perfume, and stale-ass alcohol. All dis shit mixed together is foul!"

Vida smacked her lips. I just knew she wanted to reply with something smart, but before she got it out her mouth, I continued. "A'ight, look, since I know y'all like to go shoppin' I'ma pay y'all to kick rocks…"

"How much?" Sheena interrupted, rubbing her palms together like she was about to hit the jackpot. "Because you know we ain't no cheap bitches."

I laughed. "Ha! Bitch, be real. Y'all the only bitches in Philly still pitchin' in on a nickel bag of bama."

Behind me, Latif and Amir stood snickering. They were enjoying the show.

"But, naw though. Sheena, peep game. Bull and Maine gon' need some things to keep them going and their minds off their case, I'ma give $500 to whoever pose nude fo' my boys."

Every broad in the house agreed to pose nude for Maine and Bull. I pulled out another wad of $5,000 and asked Sheena what she had left from the 5 gees I had given her earlier.

She replied, "About half."

"Okay. Take the rest of dat and put it on Maine's and Bull's books."

I opened all the windows in the house myself. I gave Latif and Amir the wad of money I had pulled out and told them to roll with Sheena and her clique. I sent them to the mall and told them to take the best shots for my boys, and whoever came up with the best pose was going to win an additional $500.

"Yo, Ock, Peewee told us to stay put," Latif said, displaying his loyalty.

I didn't wanna over-ride Peewee's order, but I needed time to think to myself. Plus, I didn't need the pussy pound in the house when Maria arrived.

"Latif, Peewee is the secretary of state. I'm the president. I could veto whoever I want. Plus, Sheena gon' leave her glock here with me, so I"ll be alright."

Latif shook his head. "Man, I don't know. That's like Secret Service leavin' the president for dead then, right?"

I chuckled. Latif was a smart young dude. I assured him that I was going to be all right. This took more than ten minutes to do, and I was actually getting frustrated with the young soldier for not wanting to leave.

When the house was finally empty, I walked to the porch and told EJ to get his drunk ass up. He looked at me and smiled before he mumbled something I could not make out. I picked him up from under the shoulder and walked him to his room, where he collapsed right on his bed. I wanted to just beat his ass. He was a waste of air. However, I laid him down and closed his room door behind me as I walked out. While I waited for Gotti B to arrive, I started straightening things out around the house.

Charles Jr. and Charlisa, my twins, were big to be only four years old. I wanted to cry, seeing them hop out of Gotti's truck and run to me. My kids had grown faster than I could ever imagine. My first born, Charles Jr., was me all over again. Even though, he was a half-breed, I knew with no doubt that he was mine.

Charlisa was my twin too, but she had hat mixed breed look that made her favor her mother more. The last time I'd seen my daughter, I just knew she was going to take on more of my African roots, but I was wrong.

After I picked them up and cradled them in my arms, I looked at Maria and asked, "What's wrong with my shawty's hair?"

Silence.

Maria didn't reply. She just walked over to me and gave me a hug. We hugged with the kids still in my arms. As we hugged, she said, "Papi, this all I ever wanted in life," and dissolved into tears.

I thought it was from the way I destroyed her life, our relationship and family, but Gotti said, "Ock, somethin' is wrong with ma. She been cryin' er' since I picked 'em up."

"And the kids don't need to keep seein' ma like dis," Timbo added. "Let me take 'em in the house."

Timbo was right. I handed him the twins and gave them kisses on the cheek. I grabbed Maria by the hand and told her to come with me. We hopped in Gotti's Range rover and I told him that I'd be back."

"Yo, B, you know Peewee gon' flip his wig if I let you roll out by yourself without any of us in tow."

My East Coast soldiers from the NY to Jersey to Baltimore feared my two West Coast lieutenants. They loved them, but feared them at the same time, especially Peewee. I guess because he had the loudest bark out of him and Black Dice. They knew he was a jokester, but they also knew he was as deadly as George Bush with a vendetta. Black Dice scared niggas by the way he looked. He rarely talked, so most niggas feared to even be around him. Black Dice and Peewee combined were like Jason and Freddy.

I lifted my shirt and showed Gotti Sheena's glock to assure him that I wasn't leaving without any protection. Me without a pistol was like a referee without a whistle. I looked at Gotti and told him, "If Peewee come back before me, in which I doubt, tell him to call me *39."

After I told Gotti what to do, Maria and I drove off. I didn't have a specific place I was headed to, so I drove to North Philly and back to west Philly. I drove back and forth from North Philly to West Philly for hours talking to Maria. As I drove, Maria explained her problems at hand. What I thought Maria was going to be talking about never came up. I thought Maria was going to come up with some kind of bullshit like, "Charlie, I need another car." Maria was a money hungry bitch, so I just knew she was schemin' on a way to get me to break bread. But, to my surprise, my baby momma had a more serious problem. She was an undercover crackhead.

When she told me she was hooked on crack, I almost ran into a fire hydrant. I felt tears rush to my eyes. God was punishing me left and right for all the bad I had done in my past. I shook my head disbelievingly and thought, *damn, how in da hell did dis bitch start usin' dope? Da fuckin' cold shit is a nigga like me is supplyin' da shit to her. Dawg, I'm destroyin' my own family.*

I couldn't focus on the road after I received the bad news, so I drove back to the house. I parked in the front and asked why.

"Maria, why did you start smokin'? Naw, fuck dat! How da fuck did you start smokin' dope?"

I tried my best to be understanding, but I was pissed. I guess she knew the more she talked the more I was going to hate her. She knew that after my mother neglected me for crack, I held low regard for crackheads. Maria thought I was going to leave her for dead, but she was wrong. I was heated, but I couldn't leave the woman who gave birth to my seeds high and dry, even if I wanted to.

I pounded my fist into the steering wheel and yelled, "Bitch, answer my goddamn question! If you want help, you gotta talk! And if I was you, I'd start talkin' now!"

I cupped her chin and lifted her head up to look me in the eyes. I snarled, "BITCH, TALK! BITCH, TALK!"

I was now frustrated and thinking about my kids. I was taking them back to Cali with me, no questions asked. Maria wasn't talking or telling me how she started smoking crack, so I snapped. Sheena's glock was pointed at her temple before I could even register what I had done. I was inches away from taking my baby momma's life.

"I'm sorry, Papi," escaped from her mouth repeatedly. "I'm sorry, Papi. Take the kids. I can't raise them like this. They need you, Charlie."

I lowered my pistol, hopped out of the truck, and slammed the door so hard Gotti and Timbo came storming out the house with their pistols dangling at their sides.

"Gotti, take dis bitch back where you got her, grab my kids some clothes, and tell dat bitch don't call me or nothin' else until she get her shit together, or whenever she's ready to talk."

After Gotti and Timbo left with my baby momma, I sat in the living room playing with my kids. Charlie was so big, he kept trying to wrestle me down. I fell to the ground and let him and his sister jump me. For the first time in years, I genuinely smiled.

"Daddy, you neva gon' leave us again, right?" Charlisa asked as she sat bouncing on my chest.

My daughter was smart. I was surprised at the way she chose her words. She was growing right before my eyes. I vowed to never miss another step of their growth.

I said, "Mami, daddy ain't going nowhere. I promise."

Looking in my daughter's eyes, I knew it was time for me to grow up and move on from the street life. I decided to fly back to L.A. and give the game up. It was time for an early retirement. I was growing tired of all the drama. I had kids to live for. Time had come for me to man up, and the first person I had to go see was Daphne. Daphne was my backbone. She was a strong woman, so I planned to do everything in my power to keep her. Behind every strong man is a strong woman, so I would be up shit's creek if I didnt make it a priority to go do what I had to do to get my woman back.

Chapter 11

Daphne

After Mya and I made it to my apartment from the comedy club, I did something with her that I'll never forget. We had sex, and 'til his day I don't know how everything went. I remember coming home and receiving another blow to my heart again. The female who called once before and called me a bitch called again. This time she didn't ask for Charlie, she asked, "Is my sperm donor there?"

"Excuse me?"

"I asked if my sperm donor was there. My sperm donor is the nigga you sleepin' with. And don't worry about my name. Just know that I'm the baby momma from hell!"

I was ready to curse this bitch out, but I got caught up with my own emotions. Tears filled my eyes like a lake. I started thinking about the female I was on the phone with. I envisioned myself doing the next female the same way this broad was doing me.

I stayed quiet, and she said, "If you let me tell it, yo' man ain't shit! You betta get away while you can before he play you like Monopoly. I don't know you, but sperm donor got ten times mo' baby mommas than you probably know about. I know dis because you don't know who I am, and I'm in L.A. That's crazy because he probably got a baby in 49 states out of 50."

She hit me with another dagger to the heart. My heart was filled with them. All I could do was sit on my bed and cry.

"Anyway, tell Charlie muthafuckin ass to watch his back. Tell him and his crab-ass homeboys that the Bloods gon' kill 'em. Them niggas may have got away with killin' my brother, but tell Charlie he gon' get his. Dat nigga killed his son's uncle with his no good ass—"

I hung up. I couldn't take no more. Charlie was a liar, cheater, deceiver, and a killer. Damn, what did I get myself into?

I sobbed and damned myself all night until I walked into the living room and woke up Mya.

"Mya, get up! I need to talk to you."

It was around 2am when I woke her up. She got up wearing nothing but her panties. When she saw that my eyes were filled with tears, she asked, "What's wrong?"

I sat beside her on the couch and said, "I gotta go. Girl, dis nigga done played me real bad. I can't stay here. I gotta go!"

I ended up explaining everything I'd learned about Charlie to Mya. I sobbed the whole time while doing so. I was hurt, vulnerable, and I needed a shoulder to lean on. Mya lent her shoulder, but she also took advantage of me.

As I leaned on her shoulder, she started massaging my tense body. "Daph, just calm down and let me massage some of dis bad energy outta you."

I didn't think anything of my best friend giving me a friendly massage during a time of stress. It didn't bother me that she was dressed only in a thong. I had also forgotten all about the comment she made earlier before we left for the comedy club.

Eventually, I agreed. I even suggested we go to my room. I was too big to be receiving a massage on the couch. Plus, it was too hard to lift my feet when she started massaging them.

We entered my bedroom and she quickly said, "Daph, don't cry. It's gon' be alright. I knew Charlie was a hoe when y'all first met, but tonight we gon' try not to think about him. Just lay on the bed and breathe slowly in and out. You gotta relieve yourself of all that negative energy. With you being pregnant, it's not good for the baby."

Mya was talking like a therapist. I asked, "Girl, when did you go to school to be a masseuse and relationship specialist?"

"Daph, I have been in yo' shoes before, remember?"

I'd forgotten all about Donte. He was Mya's first and only boyfriend. He did her bad. When she was twelve, he took her virginity then messed over her. This was before she matured and dedicated herself to school and running track.

When Mya turned thirteen, she was already two months pregnant by him, but due to him cheating on her and playing with her emotions, she had a miscarriage.

Thinking about Mya's life changing events, I thought she'd probably know a little something of what she was doing. I went along with her program. I needed something to knock me out of my nightmare, so I let Mya do her.

"Daph, since you can't lay on your stomach, I need you to take off yo' gown."

Under my nightgown, I only had on some panties. She was now massaging my feet and doing a hellava job. It was so soothing. I took off my gown and she started putting baby oil on my feet.

The next thing I knew, she had my legs spread eagle. She started massaging my inner thighs and I forgot all about my issues with Charlie. I moaned softly as she touched me in a way I couldn't touch myself. The touches were so sensitive and felt so good, it was scary.

As she massaged up and down my legs, I asked her, "What are you doing?" I was foaming at the mouth, becoming wetter by the minute. This was not supposed to be going down. I wanted to tell her to stop, but she was making me feel too good.

She ignored my question and kept going. I knew what she was doing was going to lead to a sexual encounter, but something in my head wouldn't let me stop her. When her hands touched the top of my thighs, I backed away, but she was persistent. This was a scary situation, yet pleasing.

My best friend was gay. She was turning me out, and I couldn't stop her. It was like half of my mind was telling me to stop her, and the other half was saying, *Girl, go all out. Yo' body need dis.*

I moaned and arched my back.

"Mya, please stop," I said, but it was too late.

She was now licking up and down my legs. My panties were dripping wet. She ran her right hand over my belly button and started massaging my left nipple. I couldn't believe myself. I was letting a woman excite me. I wasn't gay, or was I?

I cried when she slid her finger inside me. It felt soo good! It was too good to be true. She was my best friend and not Charlie. But, whatever she was doing with her fingers felt ten times better than when Charlie stuck his fingers in me.

I was enjoying the pleasure so much I helped remove my panties. She then penetrated my lake with three fingers, and I couldn't be still. "Oh my Gawd! Oh my Gawd!! Oh my Gawd!" I yelled as she went to work with her fingers.

I started massaging my nipples as she pulled her fingers from inside me and put them in her mouth.

"Mmmmmm! Girl, you taste good." She said as she licked my cum from her fingers.

She buried her face between my legs, and before she started licking my pussy, she blew on my asshole. I was in La-La land.

Mya ended up sucking my pussy from one end to the next. I nutted so many times, I lost count after five. Afterwards, I felt bad, but nothing was worse than the situation I was already in.

I told Mya, "I don't know what just happened, but dis is only a one time thing. I should be mad at you for takin' advantage of me, but I gotta thank you for givin' me the opportunity to test both sides of the water."

Mya didn't seem to mind that I was telling her that I'll never let her turn me out again.' She stuck her finger back in my snatch and said, "Lick your cum off my fingers, and I'll consider us even."

She stuck her finger in my mouth, and I did as told. I licked my cum off her fingers.

Mya was really trying to turn me into a lesbian, but I made it clear that I was strictly-dickly. I told her, "Our sexual experience was a mistake on my behalf."

Although she took advantage of me during a bad time, I told her she could still be my best friend, but she did not like my answer.

Later that day, after we washed up and got a few hours of sleep, I dropped her off in the projects. When we made it to her unit, she said, "You'll get over Charlie one day. He's a hoe. That's why I don't fuck with niggas. They janky."

Mya hopped out my car, shut the door, and stuck her head in the window. "The rainbow community is a nice community to live in or come to visit. Think about it. Bye!"

"Damn, Daphne, you done got grown on me. You pregnant and everything. Girl, the last time I saw you, you were in here with yo' momma. That was about five years ago. Shit, my husband was still alive about that time," my hairstylist, Shante said.

After dropping Mya off at home, I decided to hit the salon. My salon since birth was Diva's Plus. Diva's Plus was located on Central Avenue and Vernon, so I took Central Avenue from the projects all the way to Vernon.

There were only four females sitting in the waiting lounge when I arrived at the salon, which surprised the hell out of me. Shante was the owner, and her husband was some famous Blood gang member who'd been killed by some Crips years back. Shante was known in the Blood community and in the Crip community as the best hairstylist in L.A. Her salon stayed crowded. If you didn't have an appointment, you couldn't just pop up. I had called Shante before I arrived, and asked if she could squeeze me in. She said, "You best come now while I'm open."

When I entered the salon, Shante acted as if I had an appointment. I cut in front of the four women that were waiting to get their hair done and hopped right in Shante's salon chair.

As soon as I sat down, Shante asked, "Girl, who done knocked you up?"

Shante was a gossip queen. I didn't want to plain out say Charlie, because there was no telling who Charlie knew or who knew of him. Charlie had lied to me so much; he could have been sleeping with any broad in the salon.

I replied, "Oh, his name is C. He's not from California. He's from New York."

"He's from the East Coast, huh?"

"Yep."

"Well, I guess that's betta than messin' with these no good ass West Coast niggaz."

"Uh-huh," Honey said, walking into the salon. She was one of the other hairstylists. "Shit, I just hooked up with some nigga from Yonkers the other day. He treated me so nice. Matter of fact, we s'pose to be goin' to the Bahamas."

One of the four broads that sat in the lounge jumped in our conversation. Her name was Keisha. She said, “I’m sorry to spoil y’all conversation on how good East Coast niggaz treat us West Coast broads, but them niggaz are just like these flamboyant-ass L.A. niggaz.”

When Keisha started talking, the salon turned into gossip city. She asked Shante and Honey, “Do y’all remember my homegirl, Shondella?”

Shante and Honey replied in unison, “Yep.”

“What about her brotha Rock Bottom?”

“Yep. We remember his ol’ jailbird ass.”

Shante and Honey were answering on key and on cue.

“Okay, do y’all remember Peewee?”

Shante said, “Girl, you know it’s damn near a Peewee from er’ hood in California. Hoe, which one you talkin’ bout?”

I sat in the salon chair quietly, but I wanted to know the same thing as Shante. Shit, was she talking about the Peewee I knew? The Peewee that hung with my baby daddy?

“I’m talkin’ bout Eric. My first love, my baby daddy! The boy I used to bring to the salon with me.

You know, the boy you said I should watch, because he thought he was God's gift to women?"

Shante blurted, "Oh, that lil' boy from Harlem Crips?"

"That's him," Keisha informed.

That's him! I also told myself as I tuned in.

"Okay, do you remember his best friend, Black Dice?"

"Yeah. That's the lil' black quiet boy."

"Shit, I heard them two niggaz doing their thang. I heard their money is long! Millionaire status. The last Crips from South Central with that status was Killa Black, his brothers, and their crews. But we all know what happened to them." Honey chimed in.

Keisha said, "Girl, you hit it on the nose. My baby daddy got so much money now it's a shame. Black Dice got money too, but they are not the ones with the real money. The person with the money is Shondella's baby daddy. His no-good-ass name is Charlie..."

Oh my Gawd! Another one. I wanted to cry, but I had to keep cool while Shante was doing my hair.

"Anyway, Charlie is from the East Coast, and he's worse than these niggaz out here. He did Shondella bad…"

Shante cut Keisha off. "Girl, who shouldn't do Shondella wrong?"

Honey added, "Huh. Somebody needed to do her wrong. Shit, she done slept with half of California."

"Well, let's say they done each other wrong. But about a month and a half ago, that East Coast nigga had Black Dice kill Rock Bottom at their mother's house. And the bad thing, them niggaz didn't even go to jail. They got so much money they paid their way up out dat shit."

"Shit, that's how the police doing it out here. You see dat nigga Rat is still out after him and Popa killed my husband. Dat nigga even just signed a distribution deal with Universal for his record company. It's crazy out here. That's why they say money talk, bullshit walk."

Damn! I thought. *Shondella is the bitch who called my house. Her son's name is Paul. She told me Charlie killed his own son's uncle. Shit is getting' crazy.*

"Oh yeah!" Keisha blurted. "Y'all know Shondella is crazy! After the police told her they're not pickin' up the case, she went around to every Blood hood in L.A. and in the valley showin' a picture of Charlie. I think if she would have had a picture of Black Dice and Peewee, she woulda showed theirs too. She's so crazy, she's puttin' a hit out on Charlie with his own money. Every week, he send her at least 2 gees, and the bitch is savin' every dime to pay somebody to whack his ass."

"So, shit, the longer he stays alive, the higher the pot, right?'

"Sumthin' like dat…"

As much as I was starting to hate Charlie, I was still in love with him. I couldn't just sit around and listen to Shondella's plan to have him killed.

I smacked my lips and asked, "Shante are you almost done?" My tone of voice let everyone in the salon know I was disturbed. However, I didn't want anyone to start guessing why I instantly snapped, so I lied. "Because I got a doctor appointment."

Shante finished my hairdo within the next fifteen minutes. I paid her and got the hell out of there.

On my way home, I decided my time with Charlie had come to an end. I needed to go back home. Charlie was my love, but he wasn't the nigga I'd thought him to be. He was too much. He told me so many lies. His name probably wasn't even Charlie. Jessica probably wasn't even his sister-in-law. She probably was one of his baby mommas. Julie and Juliet were probably his daughters, and Miss. Warner probably wasn't his mother. Chocolate and Joyce weren't his sisters, and he probably had AIDS after what I'd heard about Shondella.

I was fed up, and tired of Charlie's shit. I didn't need to put up with his lying ass, and I didn't need any drama in my life. I was only fifteen! The bad thing was, I felt like my mother. I fell in love with a no-good-ass nigga. I fell for his trap. Like my mother wanted to leave my father but couldn't, I wanted to leave Charlie, but couldn't.

A hard head makes a soft ass. I wished I had listened to my momma. I was in love with lies. I was in love with a fake, a counterfeit, and a foul-ass nigga. But the funny thing, I couldn't shake Charlie's dog ass if my life depended on it. The lies he fed me had me hooked.

When I made it home and started packing my belongings, my cell phone rang. I answered on the second ring.

"Yo, I'm glad you answered. Daphne, ma, I apologize for not tellin' you off the back. Shawty, I know I got a lotta explainin' to do. I just got off the plane. I couldn't stay in Philly after Jessica called me and told me what happened..."

Charlie started explaining himself, but I hated talking to him over the phone. I wanted to see his facial expressions. I wanted to see if he was being truthful or telling another lie.

I looked at the suitcase positioned at the foot of the bed full of clothes and snarled, "Charlie, as much as I wanna believe the things you tell me, I can't! You lied to me so much, I don't know what to believe. I got my clothes already packed, so if I'm not here when you get home, don't bother to call me."

"Daphne, ma, don't do me like dat. I love you, shawty! I'm willin' to give up er' thin' fo' you..."

"Daddy, is that your girlfriend? Can I talk?" Charlie was cut off by a little girl in the background.

Charlie handed her the phone. She said, "Hi!" She sounded so angelic and polite. I wanted to cry. Tears rushed to my eyes.

I replied, "Hi! What's your name?"

"Charlisa. I'm four-years-old. Are you my daddy girlfriend?"

I didn't know what to say. I didn't know where I stood with Charlie. I thought I was his fiancé, but after talking to Charlene and Shondella, I didn't know what to think. And putting two and two together, who was Charlisa's mother?

"My daddy told me you guys are getting married. He told my brother and me that you going to be our stepmother. Is he telling the truth?"

Yeah, dis child belong to Charlie, I told myself. Charlisa was smart just like her father. She was questioning me like she was grown. I didn't know if Charlie was telling her what to say or not, but if he was, he was getting what he wanted, because Charlisa had me feeling mixed emotions.

I mean, I didn't want to hurt her feelings by saying, *No. Your father is a liar! A cheater! And you got mo' brothers and sisters than you know about.*

However, I said, "Yes. Your father is tellin' the truth. I'm going to be y'all stepmother. But, first, what's your brotha name and how old is he?"

"My brotha name is Charles. He's my twin. He wants to talk to you too. Want to talk to him?"

Shit was happening fast. Charlie had twins! He had a junior! And he had a daughter smarter than any four-year-old I'd ever met. I didn't know how to react. I didn't know how to accept my nightmare/dream. I'd always wanted to be happily married to the man who took my virginity and have a big family. My nightmare was getting played by Charlie and finding out that he was just like my father.

Charlisa gave Charles Jr. the phone and he asked the same question as his sister. "Are you my daddy's girlfriend?"

"Yes."

"Are you mean?"

"No."

"So you nice?"

"Yes."

"You gon' be my girlfriend too?"

"I can't be your girlfriend if I'm already your father's girlfriend."

"Yes you can! My momma was my girlfriend and my daddy's girlfriend."

Damn! That hurt. If only the baby knew what he'd just started. But thank you, Charles Jr. You just let me know dat yo' cheatin' ass daddy is still fuckin' with yo' momma.

"My momma calls me and my daddy her papi…"

"Man, give me dis phone," Charlie said, grabbing the phone from his son. "I'm already in trouble, you gon' get me in some mo' hot water."

"Daddy, why are you in hot water?" Charlisa asked.

"Lisa, Daddy in hot water because I lied to Daphne about you and your brotha. But Daddy on the phone right now, so hol' on."

Charlie directed his attention back to me. "Hello!"

"What?" I snarled as if I didn't want to be bothered.

He said, "Daphne, look, since I see you don't wanna be bothered with me and kids, just do what you feel is best. If you not home when I arrive after you see I've told my kids all about you, I'll let 'em know that you don't love us."

Charlie was playing mind games with me again. He was using his intelligence to outsmart me. He was so smooth with it, putting his kids in the mix and putting words in my mouth.

I didn't want to be the bad guy to his kids, especially Charlisa. I was really liking little momma. I said, "Charlie, I'll be here when you get home. You get one chance to explain everything. I'll make my decision after that."

Charlie replied, "That's a deal," and hung up.

Chapter 12

Charlie

I was back in Los Angeles less than 24 hours after I'd taken custody of the twins from Maria. I'd waited half the night for Peewee and Black Dice to return from their mission. When they arrived, Peewee told me how it all went down…

Fat Rat was as dead as a doorknob once I sicced Peewee and Black Dice on him. When all was said and done, my two West Coast lieutenants had made the Philly homicide rate skyrocket. They were trained killers.

I remember the day I met them. They were in a stolen car driving around L.A., ready to kill something. They pulled up on me with their pistols pointed.

"Cuzz, where you from?" Peewee had asked, hanging out of the driver window.

"The East Coast," I'd replied, not knowing that if you say you're from the East Coast in L.A., people would automatically assume you are a Crip.

Peewee countered, "Aww Cuzz! That's right! What they call you?"

To make a long story short, I met Peewee and Dice while they were out on the prowl. I was immediately fascinated with the way they displayed their gangsta mentality to me. After they found out I wasn't a Crip, Peewee said, "Man, you gotta learn a lot about the West Coast, or somebody gon' kill you. I mean, if we were Bloods and you told us you're from the East Coast with all dat blue on, you'd be dead."

I started hanging with Peewee and Dice every day after they explained all the dos and don'ts of the West Coast to me. After a month of hanging with them, I introduced them to JR. He immediately said, "Put 'em on the team."

Eventually, I would learn why JR decided to recruit Peewee and Black Dice. He knew if they ate and we treated them well, they would be loyal. They were loyal to the Crips but wasn't eating, so JR figured if he fed them and let them eat off the plate, they would eventually be more loyal to us down the line. The gamble paid off.

JR bought Black Dice and Peewee's loyalty with an initial investment of $50,000. On the West Coast, people couldn't look at my brother or I without Peewee or Dice wanting to kill them. However, in Harlem is where I made everything official. This is where I learned that my two West Coast friends were more than just gang members; they were killers.

In Philly, they took Ralph, Homicide, and Lady with them. They used the screwdriver from out of EJ's house to steal a car. Peewee was a professional at this. After he committed a GTA, he had Ralph follow him and Dice in it. They drove to the Northside.

Fat Rat owned a barbershop that he used as a business front for his illegal activities on the Northside of Philly. Peewee parked Gotti's Denali three blocks away, kept the engine running, commanded Lady and Homicide to stand guard, and he and Dice walked around the corner and hopped in the stolen car with Ralph.

Ralph drove two blocks over and parked across the street from the barbershop. Peewee took in the scenery and said, "Dice, there's a back and front entrance. How do you wanna do dis?"

Dice found a hole in Fat rat's security immediately. He spotted Fat Rat off top seated in a barber chair talking to a few of his soldiers. Rat was 25, so Dice knew the young dudes around him were nothing but pawns.

The security defect that Dice snap-finger-fast recognized was that Fat Rat left both of his shop doors open. He saw that he could run in through the front door and out the rear. He shook his head and smiled. "Cuzz, dem niggaz got guns, but we can get 'em easily. We gone come through the back..."

"Hol' on." Peewee cut Dice off. "Look! We gon' let ol' Ralph get his shine on. We come through the back and have him park in the front diagonally. If anyone run outta the front door, Ralph will get to put his trigger finger to work. Nah mean?"

"Gotcha."

Peewee was the commander in chief. After he told his two counterparts their roles, he told Ralph to pull off. Ralph did just that. He drove to the rear of the shop and Dice and Peewee leapt from the car. Ralph then drove back to the front of the shop. But before he did that, Peewee told him, "When you get to the front, park the car where we could hop right in. But do not. DO NOT Park where you'll be in the middle of the crossfire. And last, but not least, stand on the sidewalk with yo' hoody on. If someone come runnin outta the shop, murk 'em. Nah mean?"

Ralph nodded. "Yep."

Peewee smirked. "I doubt anyone will make it out, but we're countin' on you just in case."

As soon as Ralph positioned himself at his post, all hell broke loose. Peewee and Black Dice entered the rear of the shop blasting. Fat Rat and his crew were caught off guard. They were so comfortable in their setting, they literally let Dice and Peewee walk into their hood, their shop, and kill everything in sight.

When they entered the shop waving semi-automatic weapons, Fat Rat threw one of his flunkies in front of him as a shield. He was scandalous like that. He did his damnest to escape death. He betrayed his boy like he did Maine and our family. However, this time he couldn't escape death. It was upon him like flies on shit.

As bullets started filling the bodies of his young goons, Fat Rat tried to run out the front door. To his luck, Ralph was a time bomb waiting to explode. He yelled, "Allah-Akbar!"

Ralph's two Barretta .9s sent slugs into Fat Rat that ripped through his upper torso, piercing his major organs. Fat Rat immediately fell to the ground and died.

Peewee and Dice came out of the shop looking like Rambos. Peewee placed his rifle at Fat Rat's temple and snarled, "Fuck you, Bitch Boy."

Brains flew every which way. The trio then walked away from the scene grinning. Revenge was the next best thing to getting pussy. Plus, our motto was, *Snitches get out in ditches, while strong niggaz smile and hit switches. Only the strong survive.*

I was elated when the trio arrived back at EJ's house. Now that Fat Rat was wiped off the face of the earth, I felt some sense of ease. The twins were asleep, and I was ready to go. I told Peewee and Dice about Maria and ordered them to grab our belongings.

"Damn, cuzz," Peewee hissed. "Shit was just startin' to get fun. Nah mean? But naw doe, on the real, what's the deal with Tracy? You cool on seein' dat bitch?"

I ended up not seeing Tracy. I didn't feel like putting up with her shit. After she didn't wanna give Sheena a number so I could reach her, I knew she was full of bullshit. I wasn't about to play the 'you see yo' son when I want you to' game, so I said, "Fuck it."

I got Charlie, Charlisa, Dice, and Peewee together and we got the hell out of Philly. Ralph drove us to the airport. As he did, I gave him instructions on his new responsibilities.

"Ralph, you and Gotti can have the East. Peewee will supply y'all. We'll set er' thin' up later. Right now, I need y'all to find out who's servin' my baby momma and put an end to dat shit. Make sure she check in a rehab or sumthin'. If she doesn't, don't trip. However, if she come to y'all tryna change, let me know."

Ralph nodded in agreement.

Fast cars, fast people, and fast food equaled L.A. Compared to Los Angeles Philly was slow. As soon as I stepped off the plane with the twins and my two lieutenants, we had to put pep in our step. Entering LAX terminal, people were moving at the speed of light.

Jessica made my day. When we made it to the lobby of Los Angeles International Airport, she held a sign that read, *Charlie Jr. and Charlisa Welcome Home.* I had the twins cradled in my arms.

To my surprise, Chalisa blurted, "There's Auntie Jessica!"

"Ma, you remember yo' auntie, huh?"

Charlisa remembered Jessica like it was yesterday. Charlie didn't remember her at all. They were two-years-old the last time they'd seen Jessica. It surprised me that Charlisa remembered her and Charlie didn't.

Jessica drove my Denali to pick us up. Once we all hopped in, she took the wheel. Peewee hopped in the passenger seat. Dice and I took to the rear where the twins sat in the middle of us. I was in awe with how Charlisa grasped things faster than Charlie. I kept asking my son if he remembered Jessica, and he repeatedly told me, "No."

I then asked Charlisa, "What do you remember about yo' auntie?"

She replied, "Daddy, I remember when Auntie Jessica took me and Charlie to McDonalds and Toys 'R' Us."

After Charlisa answered my question, I started wondering if Charlie was a little slow. Was he missing a few screws, or was Charlisa simply smarter than him?

"Choo, you gotta realize that we all perceive things differently. Just because your junior don't remember me, and Charlisa do, don't mean he's slow or retarded. She probably enjoyed our time together so much, she just never forgot. Charlie probably didn't enjoy it as much as Charlisa did, and it was just another day to him. Also, remember they were only two, and in all honesty, I don't think Charlisa is an average four-year-old."

I was thinking the same thing. Was my princess a genius or something? I didn't know, but I was going to find out.

As I thought about the kids, Dice said, "She's a winner."

Dice surprised me. He hadn't said a word since they laid Fat Rat down in Philly.

"Man, get ready to send her to college before she turn thirteen."

I smiled. "Yeah, I see."

I felt good after Dice made his comment. For the first time in a long time, I was able to feel good about being a father. I asked Dice, "Nigga, when you gon' have kids?"

"Shit, being next to the twins makes a nigga like kids right now," he replied. "But seein' all the shit you go through make a nigga think twice. Also, before I bring some kids into dis world, I gotta retire from dis street life. I'm not tryin' to talk down on the shit we do, but it's not somethin' I will want my kids to see."

"Dice, I know that's right," Jessica added. "You're the only one in this car with some kind of sense."

I didn't reply to what Dice said. Right was right, wrong was wrong, and I was wrong. How I was living my life and being a deadbeat father, I was wrong as two left shoes. I couldn't respect myself for the way I was handling my fatherly duties.

Black Dice continued. "Homie, I do dis for the hood, for the love of the block, and for the love of y'all. But what I was sayin' about the kids is dat they are the ones who get fucked the most. I was reading the LA Sentinel when I was in the hospital. One of the staff writers was talkin' about our generation of black folks and how the generation under us will continue destroyin' our people with broken homes and genocide."

Dice was going into some deep stuff. Peewee nor I wanted to hear it. We both came from a broken home. We knew how it felt not to have a parent at home. Dice didn't. Both of his parents, and his grandparents raised him. It showed in a major way. One thing that stood out the most was he respected all women and his elders. I rarely heard Dice call a woman a bitch or hoe. He called black women sistas and other women by their names. Unlike Peewee and I, we called all women bitches and hoes.

Peewee cut Dice off. "Crip, we don't wanna hear no black political shit, cuzz."

Jessica pulled into an Arco gas station with a McDonalds in it. She looked at Peewee and me and screwed her face. "Y'all need to listen. Shit, Peewee, we know how many babies Choo has, so how many you have?"

"Just three."

Jessica laughed. "Ha! Boy, you say that like three kids isn't a lot!"

"Shit, it ain't! Compared to Choo, I'm doing just fine. Plus, I keep my bitches in pocket. Choo is a passive nigga. I'ma nigga who'll slappa bitch. Choo let his baby mommas get away with murder. I don't let a bitch get away with shit! A bitch can't even look at me wrong."

Peewee was right. His baby mommas, Keisha, Ashley, and Karen all respected him. I guess it was because he treated them like shit. I'd never seen Peewee have any baby momma drama.

I, on the other hand, was getting sent to hell and back by baby mommas. I'd never treated them bad or put my hands on them, and I was getting treated like I wasn't shit. They were putting me through drama on the daily. I obviously didn't mind the drama, because I was still bringing kids into the world.

I looked at Dice and said, "Dawg, I just need to figure sumthin' out. Outta all the bitches we've fucked, I ain't never really seen you fuck none. Dice, what is it? Because it's crazy dat you're the only one outta the crew dat don't have no kids. I'm startin' to second guess you. Yo, you ain't on no down low shit, are you?"

Dice shook his head. "Dis is why I let you and Peewee do all the talkin' sometimes. You and Motor Mouth say and ask some dumb ass shit…"

"Awww nigga!" Peewee started. He became argumentative, which was one of his downfalls. "Awww nigga, who is you to say what tha fuck we say and ask be some dumb-ass shit?"

I knew Peewe was about to take our simple conversation to another level. Jessica knew the same thing. She parked next to a pump and told the twins, "Come on."

After the kids and Jessica hopped out of the truck and walked into the McDonalds, I asked, "Who hood are we in?"

We were on the corner of Prairie and Century Blvd. The Hollywood Park Casino and Race Track was across street. I knew from the blue spray paint that I'd seen on a liquor store up the street, that we were in Crip territory. However, I wanted to prevent Peewee and Dice from getting into it over a simple debate. Plus, in L.A., it was like every other block was someone else's neighborhood.

Peewee replied, "Choo, don't start actin' dumdfounded. Cuzz, as much as we come to dis gas station, you already know who hood dis is. Man, you only live about three miles away from here. How the fuck you don't know who hood dis is?"

"See, cuzz, that's why I don't say shit around yo' big mouth-ass," Dice scolded. "All you had to say was dis 102 Raymond Crip hood."

I just shook my head when Dice finished his statement. I had never seen or heard him snap so quickly. I guess at times, Peewee could wear on the nerves of the humblest person.

To my surprise, Peewee didn't contest Dice's statement. He simply said, "Look, homie, I'm not even 'bout to bite. I'ma let chu finish tellin' us why you ain't got no kids."

Silence.

Dice ignored Peewee. He knew how to be quiet when he needed to be. He just looked out the window shaking his head. I hated when Dice snapped into this mode. Believe it or not, the nigga was scary when he became mute.

I tried to defuse the situation with sarcasm. "Yo, so you get mad at yo' best friend and take it out on er' body? Nigga, me and you were talkin'."

A snide grin spread across Dice's face. He didn't say one word. I thought, *man, dis nigga Dice have gone completely crazy. Dawg, I'm the muthafuckin boss! I run dis shit. What's wrong with dis nigga?"*

"Aiyo, I thought I was the one who run dis shit. Dice, I need to know where yo' head at, homie. Man, a nigga can't have you always makin a nigga have to guess if you all right or not."

Dice looked me over and shook his head. "My nig, shit ain't the same! Peewee, we ain't no grimey street niggaz no mo'. You need to stop actin' like a kid. Crip, grow up! Man up! Nigga, you's a million dollar nigga. Crip, look where we at and where we come from… Crip, what I'm sayin' is, it's time to move on with our life. It's time to grow up. I don't know about y'all, but I'm cool on dis bullshit ass lifestyle. I was going to retire when I reach five million in my stash, but the three I got will work. I'm cool on dis! After today, I'm movin' on."

I wasn't surprised to hear Dice announce his retirement. I sensed when he was teaching me how to read stocks that the streets weren't for him anymore. However, Peewee was in a state of shock. He was a full-fledged gangbanger and couldn't see himself or Dice retiring anytime soon. He felt betrayed. I was glad we were fresh off a flight, because there were no pistols around. We'd left all our guns in Philly. After 9-1-1, airport security was tight as virgin pussy.

To Peewee, Dice wasn't supposed to retire at such a young age. He felt Dice was trying to leave him for dead.

"Cuzz, how in da hell you just gon' try ta leave a nigga? Fool, dis shit iz fo' death doe."

Dice shook his head. He knew his best friend would not understand. Peewee didn't wanna grow up. It was like the streets had a lock him.

"Cuzz, if y'all two niggaz don't see dat our shit iz on the brink of falling, y'all some stupid-ass niggaz. No disrespect, Charlie, but since JR died, our whole organization has been on a downward spiral. You got baby momma drama that's fuckin' er' thin' up. Peewee doin' shit without even usin' his head. I'm takin' bullets becuz y'all niggaz wanna fuck just about any woman. Choo, you don't care who you fuck without a condom.

You got four girls pregnant, all stayin' in one apartment complex. Peewee, I love you, my nigga, but Ashley, Keisha, or Karen gon' kill yo' ass one day. Dawg, you stay beatin' em' like runaway slaves.

"Y'all got baby momma drama! Er' time somethin' happen, it's over y'all and some kind of dick and pussy shit. Niggaz, we just lost Maine, Bull, and Bunch over some baby momma bullshit. We all know if Shondella wouldn't have pulled dat stunt she pulled, Maine and 'em wouldn't have went OT."

Dice was throwing daggers at my heart, but truth be told, he was right. I wasn't running the empire right. Shit was falling apart with me at the helm. I couldn't knock what he was saying. His reasoning for retiring was good with me. All I could do was respect his call. Quiet as kept, I was ready for retirement too, but I was caught in the web.

I told Dice, "Man, I know how you feel. I can't lie to you, if my brotha was still alive, you wouldn't have to be doin' all dis extra bullshit I got you doin'. I respect yo' decision, homie, and truthfully speakin', I'm right behind you."

"WHAT?" Peewee blew his cap. "Awww cuzz! Charlie, you been plannin' to shake me too? Aww cuzz! Fuck you niggaz!"

Peewee was hot. He felt that Dice and I had both betrayed him. He hopped out of the truck and scowled, "Fuck you sucka-ass niggaz. Cuzz, I'm outta here. I'm not rollin' witch y'all scary-ass niggaz. I'm 'bout to call my baby momma, I'm outta here."

As he hopped out of the truck, Jessica and the kids were coming back with bags of food in their hands. Peewee immediately waved down a taxi coming out of the Hollywood Park Casino.

Dice called him by his real name to make him come back. "Eric, cuzz, you trippin'."

Peewee countered as he got in the cab, "Naw, nigga, y'all trippin'!"

"What's wrong with Peewee?" Jessica asked walking up.

I shook my head. "I don't know."

"Daddy, where is Uncle Peewee going?"

Damn! My daughter was aware of everything. I told her Uncle Peewee was going to handle some business. I didn't feel right lying to my daughter, but I had to.

Dice took it upon himself to answer Jessica. "What's wrong is dat Peewee is not ready to grow up. He gotta learn he can't be Super Crip forever. He gon' learn the hard way, just like Maine."

After Peewee's cab driver smashed off, Jessica handed us our breakfast combos. She hopped back into the driver seat and asked, "Now, where we headed?"

"I gotta go see Daphne," I said.

"Jess, you can drop me off in the Valley," Dice informed. "I pulled a nurse while in the hospital. She stays a couple miles from my mom's house, and about four miles from yo' house."

Mrs. And Mr. Lee stayed in the same Valley as Jessica, so I told Jessica to drop me off in Hawthorne. From where we were, my Hawthorne apartments were only a few miles away. As we drove, I told Jessica everything Maine told me he wanted her to do in Miami.

When we got to 134th Street and Yukon, Jessica parked. I decided to call the house phone to make sure Daphne was still home. I didn't want to go looking for her at her father's crib or the projects, but I had my mind set on the fact that if need be, I would.

After the second ring, Daphne answered. I became elated. *Thank You, Gawd,* I silently praised. However, she wasn't too elated to hear from me. She didn't want to talk to me, so I was blessed when Charlisa out of nowhere asked to talk to Daphne.

I had told my daughter all about Daphne on our flight back to Los Angeles. With the way Charlisa articulated words, I decided to let her talk. My daughter was a complete blessing from up above. She got the job done.

There was no way I was going to let Daphne move out of my life that easy. When the kids and I walked into the apartment, she already had all her belongings bagged and packed. I decided to flip the script. I knew she was mad at me, but I had to play her anger against her.

The twins pleasantly surprised me. They ran straight to Daphne and gave her a hug like they knew her. Daphne smiled. A side grin spread across my face as I thought of my next move.

"Yo, ma, what tha hell wrong with cha? I don't care how mad you are! But why the fuck was you carryin' these heavy-ass bags? Ma, you must ta forgot you carryin' my seed?"

Daphne cut her eyes at me. "Charlie, don't make shit any worse, okay? Because you's da hoe who messed up. Not me!"

"Daddy, what did you do?" Charlisa asked.

"Yeah, tell us all what you did, Charlie," Daphne added, placing her hands on her hips. "I think it's best to get it all out while I feel like listenin'. Shit, matter of fact, do the twins even know about their other siblings?"

I shook my head. "No."

I ended up explaining everything. However, I didn't mention Chocolate, Joyce, or Mo'nique. I felt I could take those secrets to my grave with me, but I was wrong. Eventually, Daphne would find out, but not this day.

As I told Daphne my situation and possible baby mommas, a knock came to my door. Of course, I didn't want to be bothered, but Charles Jr. hopped out of Daphne's lap and yelled, "Who is it?"

Things were happening so fast. I didn't realize that Daphne and I had taken a seat on the sofa with one the twins in each of our laps. We looked so lovely together; I wished I had a camera to savor the moment.

After Lil' Charlie yelled, "Who is it?" I followed him to the door. When I opened the door, it was Chocolate. I did not want to see her, especially not at this moment.

"Chocolate, I'm handlin' some business. I'll be down there later."

"Well, you seem to always be busy when it comes to me. Charlie, I ain't goin' to keep doin' dis shit. Plus, I didn't come to talk to you. I came to talk to Daphne."

I gave Chocolate the evil eye. She was trying to play me. I sensed she was becoming jealous of Daphne and what she and I had going. And what tha fuck she need to talk to Daphne about?

"Yo, we're busy! But what's so important dat you gotta talk to Daphne?"

Shit was getting out of hand and unpredictable. Chocolate smiled, leaned toward my ear, and whispered, "I just came to put yo' lesbian on blast."

My eyes widened. This shit was becoming more complicated than I'd ever thought. I asked myself, *Yo, what is dis bitch talkin' bout? Is dis bitch tryna say Daphne gay?*

Daphne leapt up from the sofa and screwed her face. "Bitch, what do you want? Don't act like we're buddy-buddy after dat shit you pulled at dat club. I'm cool on you bitches."

I arched my brows. "What club?"

Strip club was my initial thought. Knowing Chocolate's history, there was no telling what club they were talking about.

"The Comedy Club. We went out the other night and dis bitch shouldn't have gone, because she can't take a joke."

"No. It's not that," Daphne countered. "It's that I hate bein' around fake bitches. And bitch, I might be young, but I'm not nowhere near stupid! I know you don't like me, so don't act like we're cool."

Look at dis shit. Jerry Springer here a nigga come, I thought as I watched the drama play out. I kept quiet, because I needed to know what the hell was going on.

"So you callin' me fake, huh?" Chocolate frowned. "Well, I'll be fake, but you gay. And did you tell Charlie?"

I arched my brows again like, 'what tha fuck?'

"Bitch, I'm not gay!" Daphne snarled.

Things were getting heated. I sent the twins to the room. Chocolate was still behind the screen door. She said, "Well, if you ain't gay, why was you and Mya suckin' on each other? Bitch, if you had any brains, you would have at least, closed yo' curtains."

"Bitch, if you weren't so nosy, you wouldn't have gotten yo' eyes busted. But I'm glad you watchin' me. Shit, I hope you like what you saw, because how I look at it, you just want what I got. You got yo' eyes on my prize, huh?"

Okay, that's enough, I thought. *A nigga don't need dis bitch, Chocolate, to slip and say she already had me.*

I chimed in. "All right. That's enough!"

To kill all the bullshit, I told Chocolate to go home. When she walked off, Daphne started explaining her lesbian affair with Mya. I was in a state of shock for an hour after she told me how she had been turned out. I wasn't mad or upset, just stunned. I think the news didn't hit me too hard because she cheated on me with a female. I mean, tell me what man doesn't fantasize about sleeping with two women at the same time?

By the end of the day, Daphne and I had talked about mostly everything I had in the closet. Thank God I had something on her, because I felt at ease telling her that there was a possibility that I was the man who fathered Chocolate's seed. Daphne didn't take this too lightly. It was once again a low blow to her, but to my surprise, she somewhat already knew.

"Charlie, don't ask how I already knew, because a woman gon' always know when her man is cheatin' on her, especially if you cheatin' on her with the girl next door."

Tears rushed to her eyes. I was glad the twins were sleep at this time, because I didn't need them seeing Daphne in such a state. I was causing a lot of pain to the woman I truly loved, and I couldn't do too much about it, because I was trying to clean out my closet the best I could.

"Daph, don't let my past break you down like dis. I know I messed up, but you're a strong young woman. Dis is why I've been changin' my ways. I love you and wanna be yo' husband. Stop cryin' and let's get past dis."

Daphne sobbed, "Charles, dis is déjà vu. I already knew. I thought I was going crazy. I thought I was just insecure. I thought everything! But I knew! I knew you were cheatin' on me. My mom even told me. I knew by the way Chocolate was actin' dat she wasn't yo' sista. I knew you were fuckin' her. My only question is, are you also fuckin' Joyce and Mo'nique? Because if you ask me, them bitches been actin funny too."

I flat out lied. I wasn't about to admit to having any sexual encounters with Mo'nique or Joyce. I mean, I would have been dumb to say, "Yeah, baby, I fucked yo' best friend."

I immediately changed the subject. "Baby, you know what?"

"What?"

"Daph, I just thought about it. I gotta get you and my kids another house. I want the best fo' you and them. Matter of fact, hol' on. I forgot to call my realtor.

I walked into the bathroom and called Jay Cooper. He answered on the first ring. I told him to find me the best property he could find in his Malibu neighborhood.

"I'll see what I could find," Jay Cooper informed. "But until then, Charles, stay out of trouble."

I agreed. "Yes, sir."

I walked back into the bedroom and told Daphne we were moving, and Jay Cooper was on the job. She was elated about getting her own house away from the Hawthorne Apartments. I had dodged the bullet once again.

Chapter 13

Daphne

Never had I dreamed of owning a mansion-sized house in Sherman Oaks, California. Charlie moved me and the twins out three days after he informed me that Chocolate wasn't his sister, just a slut he fucked on a few different occasions, and it was a chance she was carrying his baby. When Charlie told me about their affair, I wanted to grab his .9mm that he kept in the closet. However, I didn't trip. Something came over me and said, *Girl, you already knew, so don't trip.*

Of course, it wasn't that easy, but when he told me he was moving me and the kids out of that apartment complex, I forgave him. I mean, life couldn't get any better than living next to A-list celebrities like Tyra Banks and Casey Kasem.

The new house sat on Venture Blvd. it had five bedrooms and four bathrooms. Each twin got their own room and bathroom. So did Charlie and me. I decided it was best to have our own bedrooms, because with his whorish ways, I was planning to lock him out of mine. He eventually turned his bedroom into an office. To my surprise, he and Black Dice had given up the street life and were buying stocks and bonds on Wall Street.

Jay Cooper took them to his tailor, and God be my witness, not one person in our neighborhood ever thought of them as ex-drug lords. They presented themselves so differently, you would have thought they'd received a complete Maury makeover.

More surprisingly, this was my last month of pregnancy and Peewee hadn't even come to the new house. I asked Charlie what was wrong with him, and he told me that Peewee was still caught up in a world of trouble. When he said that, I knew they were mad at each other.

I was truly enjoying my new lifestyle and the new lifestyle Charlie and Dice were living. I didn't know why they decided to just give up their empire, but I did know a lot of shit was happening. Like after I told Charlie what I heard at Diva's Plus from Peewee's baby momma, he called Peewee and warned him to be careful around Keisha. However, Peewee was so upset with Charlie and Dice for retiring from the street life, he told Charlie to kiss his ass.

Peewee was acting real stupid to me. I couldn't understand why he didn't want to follow Dice's and Charlie's lead. They had been a team for so long, it was surprising that he didn't want to join. And what made things worse, he honestly stuck to his word. Charlie figured after a few weeks of thinking about it, Peewee would realize the urgency of switching their style, but Peewee never did. After two months of not seeing Peewee, they started conducting business without him.

While I was living out a dream in Sherman Oaks, the three Dixie Chicks in Hawthorne started dropping their loads. Chocolate was first. She had a girl, and had the nerve to name her Charnay Warner. I swore I wanted to slap the shit out of that girl.

Joyce had a girl too. She went into labor two weeks after Chocolate. Her daughter was two months premature. She named her La'joi Joyce Warner, which gave Charlie away. He fucked her too.

Charlie was out fishing with Jay Cooper, Dice and some famous white actor when I found out Joyce's daughter's name. Mya called and told me that Mo'nique had told her. Over the course of time, the three of us had all gone our separate ways. Our friendship was damn near over. We all had our own problems, and even though Charlie never admitted it, I just knew Mo'nique had slept with him.

I waited for him to arrive home from his fishing trip to drop the bomb. The twins were buried in his chest when he walked through the door, and I was buried in his ears.

"Nigga, you lied again!" I scolded.

He had the nerve to sigh and say, "Yeah, I know."

I could've had a heart attack. It stopped then started pumping frenetically. I couldn't control myself.

"You no good! You scandalous! You don't care if you bring home AIDS! Man, I'm getting tired of dis day to day bullshit! Charles, the birth named her daughter La'joi Joyce Warner!"

I started crying. I couldn't even go off like I wanted to. I put myself in that situation. I had too many warnings. It wasn't his fault, it was mine. What was I doing wrong?

I immediately stopped going off. There was no way I was putting up with Charlie. I took off my engagement ring and threw it at him, and then I turned on my heels and headed straight to my room. After locking the door behind me, I started packing.

This nigga got me twisted. I know I can do better. Or can I? They say all niggaz are cheaters, so Charlie probably does love me, but he can't stop cheating. Should I leave and go find me an adventurous woman? Shit, I did love how Mya pleased me. A woman might know how to treat me better.

I was losing my mind. There I was thinking about going lesbian. Now I see how some men drive females to each other. I only had one man in my life, and he was slowly pushing me to the rainbow community.

As I stood thinking to myself and packing my belongings, Charlie knocked on the door.

"Daphne, let me talk to you."

I ignored him.

"Shawty, I know you hear me. I'm tellin' you, dat baby ain't mine. We gon' get a test."

He seemed agitated. I'd heard the 'he ain't mine' saying once too many times. He said the same thing about Chocolate. He also went as far as saying she used to sell pussy before he met her. I didn't believe nothing he said.

I yelled, "Leave me the hell alone, you fuckin' cheater!"

My stomach started hurting. For some reason, my son started kicking. I think he was taking sides with his father. I stopped packing and lay on the bed. I placed my hands around my stomach and begged my son to stop kicking.

I ignored Charlie at the door and cried for over an hour. My stomach was killing me. I was exhausted. As I laid in the bed sobbing, I grabbed the remote to my sound system and started listening to Mary J. Blige's song, "Not Gone Cry."

I needed some strength as a woman. I needed strength to get up and leave, but I couldn't find it. I was too lost in love to say, 'enough is enough.' And I was too attached to the twins. If loving Charlie was wrong, I didn't wanna be right.

Charlisa knocked on my door as "Not Gone Cry" went off.

"Mommy, can I come in your room with you?"

The twins had started calling me mommy, which I loved. Their real mother was too gone off crack, so I was their mother. It caught me by surprise how fast I'd fallen in love with Charlie's kids, especially Charlisa. I loved braiding her hair and picking out her clothes. She was the reason Charlie and I stayed together at times.

I got up to let her in, and it seemed like all the kicking in my stomach stopped. When I opened the door, Charlisa hugged my waist. She was my new best friend. I had lost everything dealing with Charlie. I wasn't in contact with my parents. I wasn't in too good of relationship with neither Mo'nique nor Mya. And my white friend, Carol, was completely out of the picture. I was rekindling my relationship with Jessica, but it was taking time. Charlisa was all I had.

Charlie Jr. was my boo too, but I favored his sister. I guess because he reminded me too much of his father.

"Mommy, Daddy in his room crying," Charlisa said. "He said you leaving us. Mommy please don't leave us."

I looked Charlisa in the eyes and they were filled with tears. I started sobbing again. Charlie wasn't playing fair. He stayed using the kids as pawns to keep me. I guess his other baby mommas used the same act on him so much, he decided to use it on me.

It worked every time. I patted Charlisa on the back and told her, "Don't cry! Mommy, ain't goin' nowhere."

For two weeks straight, I ignored Charlie. When I got up each morning, I cooked for me and the kids. I stayed in my room until he and Black Dice left to go to Jay Cooper's office. After they would leave, I'd come out of hiding and get the kids dressed. They weren't in school yet, so I'd take them to the playground or something. Charlie made it home around five o' clock most days, so we'd always make it home about four so I could start cooking. But just like breakfast, the kids got fed and his food was either in the refrigerator or on the stove.

Exactly two weeks after Mya called and told me Joyce gave birth, she called again and told me Mo'nique gave birth to a boy. The first thing I asked was, "What's his name?"

"Maine Jacob, Jr."

I breathed a sigh of relief. At least the baby's name didn't start with a C. I felt bad for even thinking my best friend had slept with my man.

"Mya, tell Mo'nique I said I'm sorry for not bein' there for her, but congrats."

After I hung up with Mya, I felt a little better knowing Mo'nique's baby wasn't Charlie's. I was relieved of so much stress, I decided to walk to the kitchen and fix Charlie a hot meal.

When he walked into the house wearing a three-piece Armani suit, I smiled, and he smiled right back at me.

"Shawty, you finally got over dat slump, huh?"

I nodded.

"Well, if that's the case, let's celebrate. I gotta surprise for you, so go get the kids ready."

"Oh my Gawd," was all that could escape my mouth when Charlie and I pulled up on Wilshire and Vermont. There was a new shopping center still under construction located west of Wilshire. I looked at the signs on the stores soon to come and I lit up with joy. Big as day was Daphne's Beauty Salon. I ignored the other signs, such as, Jessica's Restaurant, JR Groceries, and Black's Enterprize Car Detail.

"Mommy, Daddy bought this for you." The twins said in unison, as if Charlie had it scripted. He escorted me by the waist from the truck to the beauty salon. Inside, everything was under construction, but the outlining of the salon was perfect. Marble walls with floor to ceiling mirrors, and ten booths with leather chairs. I pranced around, touching and feeling everything. I was so surprised and excited, I couldn't stop saying, "Thank you."

As I glanced over the whole salon, I mumbled, "Dis is adorable."

No doubt, the salon was adorable, but like always, Charlie's cell phone went off, spoiling the mood. He answered on the first ring. "Yo. Jess, can you hit me back."

Immediately, my ears perked up to catch his end of the conversation. I trusted nothing about him now.

"Aww damn! How did you do dat?"

"You said all of 'em?"

"Damn, that's good!"

"Are they straight?"

"It ain't no shit yet, is it?"

"Jess, I don't believe you pulled dis shit off."

While he was on the phone, I stood directly in front of him with my hands folded across my chest and tapping my left foot on the floor. I knew as soon as he said, "Well, I'm on my way," that our special event was over.

"Give me about an hour, I gotta drop Daphne and the twins off at home, and I need to pick up Dice."

My son started kicking as soon as his father finished his statement. I twisted my face from the pain and put my hands over my belly. "Boy, please don't start," I mumbled.

"Ma, you all right?" Charlie asked after he hung up.

I looked at him with a frown. "Just take me and the kids home, so you could attend to your more important business."

I didn't know why it was so urgent that Charlie made it to Jessica's house, but I was tired of being put on the backburner.

"Baby, I'm sorry, but dis is very important."

I ignored him and walked back to the truck. As we drove back home from L.A. to Sherman Oaks, I was hurting everywhere. From my heart, down to my stomach, down to my feet. When we made it home, I grabbed the twins by their arms and said, "Come on."

Charlie just put his head on the steering wheel as we walked in the house.

That night after Charlie left, my son was kicking so much I slept in the living room with the kids. I cried all night. Charlie was playing me in more ways than one. I wanted to just up and leave him, but I couldn't. He had me by strings like a puppet master. I felt just like my mother.

I fell in love with a nigga who I thought I knew, but truth be told, I didn't know shit about Charlie. Every other day I learned something new about his dog ass. I cried my heart out. My son wouldn't stop kicking. I'm glad the twins were asleep. They didn't need to see me go through so much pain, or did they?

Chapter 14

Charlie

I showed up at Jessica's house ten minutes early with Dice in tow. I wished Peewee was there with us. Jessica had pulled the unbelievable. She had all my baby mommas in one house. Even Chocolate and Joyce attended. More surprisingly, drama queen Shondella even showed up.

When Dice and I entered the house, all eyes were on me. It was as if we'd walked into a room filled with venomous snakes. My kids were there too. Their ages ranged from 3-years-old to 2-weeks-old.

My nieces were the first to approach me. Julie said, "Uncle Choo, all your kids are here." She smiled at me like she knew what was going on.

Juliet added, "And their mommas are all mad at you."

I just shook my head. It was amazing how fast my nieces picked up on everything. I gave them a hug and kissed them on the forehead to relieve some of the stress that was coming over me. Having my five baby mommas staring at me with hate in their eyes scared the shit out of me.

To my luck, my mother and Jessica were two strong intelligent women. They had everything set to a T. I told myself, "Damn, I'm glad I got some help. Thank you, God."

I was surprised that all my baby mommas didn't just kill me on sight. They just sat mean mugging like I was a snitch at a gangsta party.

Momma said, "Okay, ladies er'body already know the rules, so please let's keep er' thin' lady like for my grandchildren's sake." My mother was slowly making her way back into my life.

Jessica met Dice and I at the door. She pulled us to the side and told my nieces to go in their rooms.

"Charlie, I need you and Dice to listen to me. Okay?"

Dice and I nodded in unison.

"Momma and I pulled the unbelievable, so we need y'all to make sure everything play out smoothly…"

I cut Jessica off. "Hol' on, Jess! I thought dis was only fo' the tests. It's almost nine, ain't no clinics open."

Jessica snapped. "If you shut tha hell up, maybe I could explain."

I stayed quiet.

"For your information, you are the only person that needs to give DNA. I paid my doctor to come and do all your baby mommas and the kids. He didn't have enough time to wait for you, so we'll get you later."

"Right now, I set up my guest room so that you can sit down with each one of your baby mommas and your maybes for at least thirty minutes. The only person who ain't here that need a test is Mo'nique. You know she's still in the hospital, so we'll do her when we get a chance."

I nodded. Jessica was my lifesaver.

"Dice, I just need you to help make sure everything run like clockwork."

Dice nodded in agreement to his assignment.

"And by the way, how's Zoe and you gettin' along?"

Zoe was a nurse Dice had met at the hospital, who was now his fiancé. I guess it all worked out for him, because within a month he asked her to marry him.

"Zoe is pregnant," Dice informed. "So we're getting along just fine."

Word? I thought. *My nigga is finally havin' a seed. Word!*

"Well, congrats, but we need to get this over with. Charlie, since Tracy and Charlene is not from out here, who do you wanna talk to first, Charlene or Tracy?"

"Charlene."

Charlene was a fly, young, educated, beauty. She was tall, thick, and firm. She had caramel skin and ebony hair. Her legs were long and attractive. I couldn't do nothing but treasure her as my baby momma. And the good thing, she wasn't drama. This why I chose to talk to her first.

"Charles, you sure do like drama, huh?" she asked entering the guest room holding my six-month-old daughter, Charlena.

I nodded in agreement, reached for my daughter, and shut the room door.

"Man, I'm tired of waitin' on dis no-good-ass nigga... Jessica, I'm bout ta leave." Shondella couldn't wait to start going off.

Charlene looked at me and took a seat on the edge of the bed. She placed her left hand on my thigh and said, "Charlie, you have issues. You've been Mr. StickYoDickInAnybody, so go handle yo' bizness."

I looked Charlene over. I knew she was one of the many women I'd done wrong. She was cool and collected. She grabbed Charlena out of my hands and said, "Go handle that."

She gave me a funny look, but I knew she was sincere.

"Go handle that." I mimicked, and walked out of the room.

I smashed my finger in Shondella's chest when I made it to the living room. I was on the verge of knocking her out.

"Bitch, why you always showin yo' ass? Didn't you learn from our last episode?"

I grabbed her by the weave and dragged her to Jessica's bathroom. Chocolate, Joyce, and Tracy were all surprised at how I flipped. They knew I was fuming, and stayed on their best behavior. These bitches were backwards. Why must a nigga express some kind of physical abuse or violence towards them to make these hoes act right?

I slammed the door after entering.

"Bitch, you just gon' disrespect my folks house like you stupid, huh? Ma, if you wanna play stupid again, I'm with it. But think of the consequences."

I was tired of Shondella's shit. I was now seriously hoping Paul wasn't my son, and after Peewee told me her background, it was a big chance that I was not his father. I was hoping like hell he was some other nigga's baby. Shit, truthfully speaking, the only female in that house that I wanted to father a child with was Charlene. I knew Charlena was mine.

Shondella frowned. "Nigga, just because you had my brotha killed, dat don't mean I'm scared of yo' bitch ass! Charlie, you got me fucked up. You and dat crab-ass nigga, Dice, betta be worryin' about the Bloods, because they gon' kill y'all bitch asses!"

"Bitch!" I snapped, grabbing Shondella by the neck and applying pressure. "Bitch, I swear, you best learn to stay in yo' place. I don't know who you think I am, but you walkin' on thin ice..."

I was filled with rage. Shondella was flirting with death. I felt her body go limp, then a big boom rattled the bathroom door as she gasped for air.

Dice had kicked the door down.

"Charlie," he called as he entered. "Man, let her go!"

I loosened my grip and Shondella fell into the tub. She was now desperately trying to catch her breath. After a moment or two of counting from 100 down to 1, I realized I was out of character. All my other baby mommas were at the door, even the kids were looking in.

I spotted Paul immediately. He was crying and caught up in the middle of his mother and my shit.

Seeing tears roll down his cheeks in rivers broke my heart.

I fell to my knees, hugged him, and told him, "I'm sorry. Daddy, didn't mean to put my hands on your mother. I'm sorry…"

When Shondella caught her breath, she grabbed Paul out of my hands and stormed out of the house. However, before she left, she hissed, "Charlie, you gon' get yours. Watch!"

Back in the room with Charlene and Charlena, I was trying to turn my frowns back into smiles, but I couldn't. I was heated. I ended up telling Charlene to go wait in the living room for me, and decided to talk to her last.

When she walked out, Tracy walked in with my three-year-old son, Tre, in tow. I forced a smile for my son, but I pissed at all their asses now. I knew his mother was another drama queen. To my surprise, she said, "I don't want chu chockin' me out, so I only got two things to tell you."

"Shoot."

"Well, first and foremost, I wanna tell you that I was messin' with like three other niggas when I became pregnant. I know Sheena probably already told you, but I do believe you are Tre's father."

I nodded. I wanted to scream at Tracy, "Bitch, why the fuck you take so long to tell me dis?" I was having mixed emotions about Tracy and my son. I didn't want Tre to have to suffer because his mother was a hoe. Although I was stuck in my own thoughts, as Tracy talked, I heard everything she was saying.

"Charles, when the test comes back in a few hours, and if you are not Tre's father, you don't gotta neva worry about me. But if you are his father, I want it all. A brand new house, car, socks, and draws."

And if I'm not his father, I want all my money back! I said inwardly. However, I kept everything to myself. I didn't want any more drama, so I let her keep talking.

"Also, I heard, Sheena is messing with Gotti, and you turned everything over to him and that lil' boy, Ralph. And Big Booty Judy got that lil' nigga sprung. All four of them been opening up shop all over the city. They even own a strip club called Pussy P."

Tracy was right. I guess she had been around Sheena or someone in Sheena's crew while they were gossiping, because she knew a little too much.

"Well, all I'm sayin' is, you helped them open up shop, now, I want you to help me open up mine."

I laughed. This bitch must be kidding me. She must've forgot she wasn't shit when I met her, and she ain't shit now.

I laughed harder, and just because I didn't like how she was getting at me, I decided Charlene was my only baby momma that deserved anything from me.

I kept laughing. You would have thought I was high off some good marijuana.

I asked, "Is dat all?"

"Hell naw!" She frowned. "And what's so funny?"

"You."

"What? I can't be like you and wear a suit? I know you don't want yo' baby momma to be stuck on the street all of her life, do you?"

I ignored Tracy. I just told her, "We'll see when the test comes back."

As she walked out of the room with Tre, I told her to tell Chocolate and Joyce both to come in. It was past twelve-thirty, I had to get home, and I still wanted to talk to Charlene again.

When Chocolate and her sister walked in the guest room with my newest creations, I just shook my head. I straight got two sisters pregnant. What was I thinking?

"Charlie, why do you want us in here together? You know I can't stand her triflin' ass no mo'. She didn't even tell me y'all was fuckin'. Then, she had the nerve to wait to have my niece, yo' daughter's sista/cousin, to tell me."

"Janet, I don't know why you trippin'," Joyce told Chocolate. "Charlie wasn't yo' man! He was fuckin' er' female in the building."

Chocolate was about to go off, but I jumped between them. "Look, I didn't belong to none of y'all. Chocolate, I told you dis off top—"

Chocolate cut me off. "That didn't give you the right to fuck my sista when you were stickin' yo' dick in me!"

"Two wrongs don't make a right," I replied. "I was fuckin' you when you knew I was fuckin' Daphne, so let's not talk about the past, because in all honesty, you seduced me."

"Okay, if you don't wanna go there, let's talk about how you gon' take care of our kids." Joyce said.

"Nigga, you need to worry about takin' care of both our babies, because I'm puttin' Joyce out as soon as we get back."

As Chocolate snarled, I looked at Charnay and couldn't help but notice the resemblance. She had my nose and lips. Even though I wanted to wait until the paternity tests came back to make any decisions, I felt Charnay was really mine. Something inside of me rejoiced.

"Chocolate, you know you can have any apartment in dat building you want, so stop trippin'! If you want Joyce outta yo' apartment, I'll give her Daphne's old apartment. I just need y'all to get along. I don't need any more drama. I mean, damn, I feel like Rodney King, can we just get along?"

Joyce was now sitting on the bed breastfeeding Lajoi. She was my only baby momma to breastfeed. I'd never seen any of my other baby mommas do it.

Lajoi was only two weeks old, so I couldn't tell if she was mine or not. I asked Joyce, "Are you sure she's mine?"

"I'm 1000% sure she's yours."

At that moment, my phone went off. I glanced at the caller ID and it was the house number. I thought it was Daphne until I flipped open the phone and said, "Yo."

"Daddy, Mommy hurt. She needs help," Charlisa cried into the phone.

I immediately heard Daphne in the background screaming. "Oh my Gawd! It's comin'! It's comin!"

"Ma'am, just breathe in and out and relax," a male voice said.

Daphne is having my son, I thought. I grabbed my keys and headed out the door.

"Charlisa, is the paramedics there?"

"Yes."

"Who called 'em?"

"I did. Mommy told me to. She's on the floor crying."

"Is the police there?"

"Yes."

As much as I hated the law, they did come in handy at times.

"Give em' the phone. Auntie Jessica 'bout to come get you and yo' brother."

An officer was standing right next to my daughter. She immediately handed him the phone and said, "My father wants to talk to you."

The officer grabbed the phone. "Hello! Mr. Warner?"

"Yes."

"Your wife is in labor. EMTs are transporting her to Kaiser off of Venice and Fairfax."

"Okay, I'm on my way to the hospital. I'm sending someone to care for my kids, but it will take her about twenty minutes to arrive."

"Mr. Warner, your neighbor would like to speak to you."

My neighbor was Jim Crabtree. I said, "Put him on the phone, please."

"Hey!" Jim said.

He was my new business partner. Jay Cooper introduced us when I bought my house. Jim was the reason I bought my house in Sherman Oaks, instead of

Malibu. He was an A-list actor in Hollywood in the late 80's. He was now an A-list businessman who owned a few studios and film companies.

"Buddy, Daphne done popped the potato. They're taking her to the hospital. I know you don't want all these people in your house, so I"ll take the kids over to play with my children until Jessica comes to get them."

I agreed. Jim told me he was going to lock up the house. I told Charlisa it was okay for her and her brother to go with Jim.

After I hung up, I left the living room, told Jessica the deal, and she said, "Charlie, dis the fourth time dis month. I'm tired of dis shit. But who house you say they were going to be at?"

I told Jessica to pick the kids up from Jim's house. I looked over at Charlene and she was sobbing. I knew she was feeling my pain. I was having baby momma drama back to back, but I was still bringing babies into this world. She knew I was addicted to sex like a crack addict addicted to crack. I wanted to just hold her tight to let her know I was all right, but I couldn't. I had to get going. I looked at Dice and said, "Come on."

To my surprise, she said, "I'm comin'."

I knew I couldn't turn her away. She was my only baby momma who actually cared. I told her, "Come on."

Chapter 15

Daphne

I didn't know I was in labor when I was lying next to the twins on the living room floor. I fought the pain for hours, but when my water broke, I knew my baby was coming.

I tried to roll over and up from the floor, but I couldn't. I was in so much pain that I didn't realize the twins were watching me. When I made eye contact with Charlisa, she asked me what was wrong.

I replied, "Lisa, call 9-1-1."

I was crying, sweating and groaning. As Charlisa ran to the phone, Charles Jr. leapt up and grabbed my hand. He didn't really know what was going on, but he moved my hair from my face and said, "Mommy, don't cry."

He then kissed me on the cheek and lay his head next to mine. He started crying with me.

"Hello! My mommy need help," I heard Charlisa say into the phone.

"I don't know. She on the floor crying. Her and my brother."

I sensed the dispatch was asking Charlisa if she knew what was wrong with me. "Tell them I'm having a baby," I groaned.

Charlisa repeated what I said to the dispatcher.

"Mommy, the man on the phone said just relax and breathe in and out until help comes."

It took the paramedics only a few minutes to get to the house, and the 9-1-1 operator stayed on the phone with Charlisa the entire time. I was almost fully dilated when they arrived, so the race was on to get me to the hospital.

As I was being placed on a stretcher, I could hear Charlisa on the phone with her father. That little girl was truly my angel. I was relieved to see our next door neighbor walk into the house as they were taking me out. I didn't know him that well, but the kids at least wouldn't be left with strangers. I couldn't ponder it too long, because the damn contractions were coming fast and furious. My son wanted out.

"Just keep breathing in and out. We see the head. He's coming!" the medic said.

I was giving birth inside the ambulance.

"Push! Push! Push!" the medics yelled.

"I'm pushin'!" I yelled back.

"He's coming. Just keep pushing."

"I'm pushin'!" I yelled again. "I hate dis! I hate the man who got me pregnant, and I'm about to start hatin' y'all ass if y'all don't hurry up and get dis baby outta me!"

I was in agony and talking trash. My son couldn't come fast enough for me.

"Push!"

"Keep pushin'!"

"The head is out. Keep pushin'."

I heard my baby whining, which let me know he was out and alive. I felt relieved and exhausted.

I don't know what happened after I gave birth. I fell asleep or something. I don't even remember making it to the hospital.

"Charlie, he's soo beautiful," I heard a lady say as I opened my eyes.

Charlie was sitting next to my bed holding our son. The lady was standing next to him with her hand on his shoulder. She was smiling like she had just hit the lottery.

I cleared my throat as I woke up to get Charlie's attention. When he turned my way, I said, "I'm mad at chu."

He leapt up from his seat and kissed me on the forehead and lips. "I already know. I heard how you were actin' a fool in dat ambulance. The medics told me."

"She wasn't actin' a fool," the lady that was with Charlie said. "She was just in a lot of pain. Givin' birth hurts. By the way, Daphne, I'm Charlene. We talked on the phone a few months back. I'm only here to support you and Charlie, and to wish you two the best. As you know, I'm not a drama queen, and I'm happy for y'all. Congrats."

I looked at Charlene and smiled. She was sincere with her approach. I didn't have any animosity towards her.

I said, "Thank you. And nice to meet you."

Just then, Black Dice, his fiancée Zoe, and Jessica walked into the room. Dice had a vase filled with flowers in his right hand and a hand full of balloons in his left hand.

"Oh, you finally woke up, huh?" he asked, sitting the flowers and balloons next to my bed.

I replied, "I didn't know I was sleep dat long. Did I even name the baby yet?"

"I did dat yesterday, ma," Charlie answered with a smirk.

"And what chu name him?"

"Charles JR Warner."

"What about Junior?" I asked. "How are you going to give both your sons the same name?"

"First off, Charles and Charlie are two different names. Second, Charlie Jr. is named after me, and our son is named after my brother."

I nodded nonchalantly. There was no reason to argue; what was done was done. Plus, I knew Charlie loved his brother, and it was a privilege for our son to be named after JR.

I lay in the hospital bed for hours talking to Charlene, Zoe, and Jessica. It seemed like Charlie and Dice drifted off into their own little world, and we drifted into ours.

Come to find out, it had been two days since I'd given birth, and the doctors weren't releasing me until they finished running tests. They had found something in my son's blood, and needed to test me to see what it was. As we were talking, a beautiful ebony complexioned doctor walked in the room holding a clipboard.

She said, "Mrs. Warner, I got some good and bad news for you. Can I talk to you alone?"

I replied, "Yes. But can my husband stay in the room with me?"

I didn't know what this doctor had to tell me, so my heart skipped a beat as soon as she said, bad news. I started thinking about my son. I prayed nothing was wrong with him.

The doctor agreed to let Charlie stay in the room.

"Mrs. And Mr. Warner, my name is Doctor Michelle R. Jones. I was the first to receive Charles Warner when the ambulance arrived..."

Dr. Jones paused. My heart skipped another beat. I sensed she was about to say something damaging before she even said it.

She was patiently tapping a pen on her clipboard. I guess, when she paused, she was reading the papers on the board and trying to figure out the best way to address the issue.

"Mrs. Warner, I don't know how to put this to you, but right before me is a consent form for HIV testing. We found something in your son's blood, and we believe you may have come in contact with the virus."

I immediately started crying. I looked at Charlie and he tilted his head toward the ground. I froze, trapped in my own thoughts, for about five minutes. I couldn't even open my mouth. HIV meant AIDS, and AIDS meant death, and I'd just given life. I was not trying to die.

"Mrs. Warner, the good news is your son tested negative for the virus, and he's in the best of health. Another good thing is law enforcement knows you are a minor and wanted to arrest your husband for statutory rape, but Mrs. Johnson and Mr. Johnson, your parents, are here. They declined to press charges."

Things were moving faster than light. From AIDS, to Charlie being arrested, to my parents finding out I was in the hospital? Then, I remembered I was still under their guardianship. *Only in America,* I thought to myself.

"Well, if you want to sign right here, we can find out if you're negative or positive."

I ended up signing. And to my surprise, Charlie said, "Well, if she's takin' the test, you might as well test me too. I'm the one who wasn't living right."

Tears rushed to Dr. Jones' eyes. She said, "The year is 2000. The date is January 17TH. AIDS first diagnosed patients were five white gay men. The year was 1981. The date was June 5th. That was exactly 18 years, 7 moths, and 12 days ago. Today, nearly 50% of new HIV cases are young black women. I hope and pray the two of you are not infected, but HIV is becoming a new trend in our community. I'm only 35, and I've seen so many of our people become infected with this virus. I'll be the first to say we need some of our people to start educating the youth about this epidemic."

I didn't know what to say as Dr. Jones stood there educating Charlie and I on the HIV virus, which causes AIDS. I started thinking about how close life and death really is.

Dr. Jones talked for almost fifteen minutes. Charlie and I were both in deep thought as she lectured. I just knew he was wondering what bitch could have given him the virus. And knowing how he was sticking his dick in every Sherry, Carrie, and Mary, it was a high chance that we were infected.

I didn't stress myself too much, because after Dr. Jones said what she had to say and Charlie and I signed all the papers to approve the hospital to give us the test, she casually walked out of the room. Then, to my surprise, my parents walked through the door. My father didn't look bothered by my situation. My mother was all smiles. Charlie just put his head between his palms and knees. I couldn't tell what he was thinking.

"So, Daphne, this is Charles, huh?" my father immediately asked.

There was no hello, how you doing, or nothing. I looked at my father and shook my head.

I thought he was going to flip out and it was going to be a problem, but he patted Charlie on the back, and said, "Hold your head, son. Life is not over. You just brought a seed into this world."

Chapter 16

Charlie

It was a good thing I decided to be cool when Daphne's father and mother walked into the room. I had heard so many dreadful stories about Mr. Johnson, I didn't know if I wanted to take him down or not. He wasn't as big as I'd thought he'd be, so I knew he was fair game.

He stood six foot two and weighed 210lbs. He was a few inches taller than me, and had me by, at least 20 pounds. I thought he was a giant. By the way Daphne had described him to me, I figured him to be Shaq's height. He didn't look big at all, but he wasn't small either. He greeted me by patting me on the back and saying, "Hold your head up, son…"

I did as told, but I wasn't too pleased knowing there was a chance of me being infected. Mr. and Mrs. Johnson were dressed to impress. They looked professional to say the least. I was glad that Dice and I were dressed in suit and tie.

Mr. Johnson said, "Charles, I don't know you, but I've heard a lot about you. I admire the way you're treating my daughter. It's hard for a young man to take care of himself, let along his girl, so I applaud you."

Mr. Johnson couldn't have been older than 45. I looked him in the eyes as he talked, and knew he was once a street thug. It was from experience that he knew what I was going through.

I began to pay more attention to him when he admitted to being just like me. He was no saint. To my surprise and Daphne's surprise, he even broke down and started sobbing. "I'm sorry, y'all! I got the virus."

Say what, now? Damn, if we're positive, Daphne could have given it to me. She could've got it from dis nigga. Shit, she coulda even got it from her gay-ass homegirl. Dr. Jones said that black women had the highest percentage of new AIDS cases.

"Damn, dis shit scary and fucked up…"

I was thinking over all the possibilities and ways I could excuse myself from being the cause. However, I was a beast who'd slept with many women who weren't clean, and I did them unprotected like it was nothing.

I looked at Daphne and she had her face between her mother's arms and chest. I wanted to go hold her, but the next thing I knew, Black Dice burst in with watery eyes. Jessica followed him with tears rolling down her cheeks in rivers. I figured they may have heard what was going on. However, that wasn't the case.

Jessica said, "Excuse me. Choo, I need to talk to you right quick. I got some bad news."

I excuse myself from the room.

In the hallway, Jessica told me, "Peewee is dead!"

I couldn't believe my ears. I replied, "What?"

Jessica repeated herself. "Peewee is dead!"

Dice nodded. "Our boy is gone." The floodgates gave way and tears covered his face.

I snapped. Before I knew it, I was heading out the hospital, not knowing where I was headed. I just had to go. Things were moving at the speed of light. My life was going downhill by the tic of the clock.

Chapter 17

Daphne

My father was unpredictable. One minute, he didn't want to talk to me. The next, he was at the hospital comforting Charlie and I. Then, the next minute, he was admitting he had tested positive for the AIDS virus.

A joyous moment in my life was overwhelmed with nightmares. I was glad the doctor had my son in another room, because the room I occupied in the hospital was not a good place for him at that moment. I excused my parents out of my room when Jessica ran into the room crying. My mother and I were getting along a little better personally, but my father was still the person making things a little hard on us, especially with his out of nowhere admission that he had been infected.

I didn't have any remorse for putting them out. I still held a grudge and animosity towards them. After all, they had just allowed me to leave their home at only fourteen years of age, without even trying to get me back. Plus, after my father said what he had to say, I just knew Charlie was going to blame me if we tested positive.

Sitting in that hospital bed made me realize how messed up my situation really was. What glittered wasn't gold. I didn't know what to do.

I was a mess.

Charlene said, "Daphne, I've been through it with Charlie too, so just know things are gon' get betta in due time."

Zoe added, "And don't let your situation stress you or get you out of your character. Remember, everything happens for a reason."

I didn't reply to Zoe or Charlene. I was stuck in my own thoughts. So much stuff was floating through my head, I didn't know what to think.

Jessica said, "Daph, when they let you out of here, come stay with me, because this stuff will drive you crazy."

Chapter 18

Charlie

Peewee was dead! I couldn't believe it. Life and death are runnin' mates, and they run too close together for me. Man, I can't believe my nigga is gone.

As I mourned the loss of Peewee, revenge was the only other thing on my mind. I wasn't a killer, but Shondella had pushed me too far. She had stuck her nose somewhere it wasn't supposed to be for the last time. Peewee had put his hands on Keisha for the last time, and she gave Shondella the go ahead to have him killed. Word had it that Shondella was patiently waiting to retaliate on me for her brother's death.

The story was not clear to Dice nor I; we just knew Shondella worked together with Keisha and had some Bloods to kill him. When we arrived in Carson, my mind flipped from everything positive I had going, to murder, murder, kill, and kill. Seeing Peewee's mother with a puddle of blood on her shirt and crying like any mother would do after losing a son, made my trigger finger inch.

Glenn, Peewee's mother, had called Dice while we were at the hospital. She told him his best friend was dead. She knew the life we lived and told Dice before we do anything crazy to come see her.

We greeted Glenn with hugs and a few consoling words as we entered her house. Glenn's house was packed with Peewee's relatives and a few of his Crip homies. Dice and I acknowledged a few of them, but Glenn led us to the shack. The shack was the same way we'd left it.

When the three of us made it into the Hideout, Glenn began to sob. "I heard it all! I was on the phone with Eric when him and Keisha got into it. Y'all know how Eric use to do dat girl and all of his baby mommas. However, this time I can honestly say, Keisha provoked dat boy. She was saying 'nigga, any other day you'll beat the hell outta me for talkin' back, so do it now'...

Glenn paused to wipe tears from her eyes.

"Then, I heard a loud smack. I thought Eric had knocked the girl out, but he said, 'aww shit! Momma, let me hit you back. Dis bitch just slapped me'. He hung up so fast I couldn't even tell him not to put his hands on that girl and come home..."

Glenn paused again. This time she started shaking her head. I guess, as she was telling us her mother's nightmare, it was really sinking in her head that her son was dead.

I'd never felt so helpless in my life. Neither Dice nor I knew what to do in this situation. We hugged Glenn again. At the same time, we said, "It's gon' be all right."

After five minutes of consoling Glenn, she went back to explaining what she knew.

"I called Eric right back after he hung up. His cell phone just rang and rang, so I knew he had flipped out on her. I called and called his phone until he picked up, which was an hour later, and he said 'momma, I done beat dis bitch ass, and now she just pulled up with some of my enemies and Charlie's baby momma. I'ma kill 'em all if they come on my porch.' I cut Eric off. He was talking too fast. And y'all know how he get when he is mad.

"I told Eric not to do anything stupid, but it was too late. He already had in his head that he was going out with a bang. I asked him how many people Keisha had with her, and he said about ten. I told him I was callin' the police. He said, 'naw! Momma, you know I'm ridin' dirty.' Then, all of a sudden, I heard gun shots ring out like the war in Iraq. It hadta been about 100 rounds or so. I just knew my baby was dead. I ran straight to my car. I called 9-1-1 while I was on my way to L.A., but I made it to the crime scene before them.

"Eric was laid in a puddle of blood on his living room floor when I arrived. He was dead!"

Glenn fell to her knees explaining the scene. This brought more of a murderous feeling upon me and tears to my eyes. I was now plotting evil against my baby momma. Shondella had gone from a drama queen to a complete snake and a threat.

"Eric's whole body was riddled with bullets, but I think he shot a few of them. I'm hoping it was that bitch, Keisha. I say this because there were trails of blood leading from the house to the streets…"

Dice and I got the news from Glenn and left. But before we left, I told Glenn where Peewee had a stash worth more than $3 million in the shack. He had a safe in the floor. I lifted up the rug and said, "The combination is Eric's date of birth. It should be over $3 million in there. Peewee never touched his money, so it might be more than that."

I had no way out of this. A woman can only push a man so far. I'd always intended to be the best baby daddy I could actually be, but Shondella wouldn't let me.

I called my mother as soon as Dice and I left Glenn's house. She answered Jessica's phone on the first ring and said, "Charlie, I'm soo sorry to hear about Peewee."

I sighed. "Yeah, I know."

I was about to ask if the tests come back, but Momma beat me to the chase.

"Charles, I got some news for you! You are not the father of Shondella's son, Tracy's son, or Joyce's daughter."

"Whoa!" I said. I was elated and couldn't believe three out of five weren't mine. Actually, I was surprised at how Joyce told me she was 1000% sure I was the father.

I was all smiles, but my good mood didn't last too long. Dice and I were on a mission, and anticipating death isn't anything to smile about.

"Momma, thank you for the news, but I gotta go."

I hung up with my mother and found myself in a darkened state of mind. Dice pulled three houses away from Shondella's mother's house and said, "Be prepared to camp out all night if need be."

We were in a stolen Dodge Ram van, so I tilted my seat and nodded my head. I was now in Dice's comfort zone, so I decided to follow the leader. We sat for hours in silence awaiting Shondella's arrival. I'd turned off my cell phone and figured Dice had turned off his until it ranf.

"Yes, Zoe."

"No. We still together."

"Yeah, he got his phone off."

"Well, if they let her and the baby go home, tell her to go with Jessica like y'all had planned. But I need you to go book us two flights up outta here, because as soon as I come home, we're jumping state to your home state."

"Okay, I'm about to cut dis phone off, because I'm in the middle of somethin'."

"All right. See you in a few."

When Dice turned off his phone, he said, "The girls were worried about you. They say Daphne is going through it, but she was worried about you and yo' wellbein'. And the doctors are releasing her from the hospital. I told them to go to Jessica's house."

I nodded. The only thing on my mind was ending my chapter with Shondella, and it happened thirty minutes after the thought crossed my mind. Keisha and Shondella pulled up in Peewee's Town Car. They had the nerve to be riding around in his car after they'd just had him killed.

As they parked in front of Shondella's mother's house, Dice started the van and said, "We lucked up. These bitches don't even know how to lay low after they snake somebody. Choo, you bout to be in your first South Central drive-by. Roll down yo' window, and when I pull up next to the car, start dumpin'."

I'd never dreamed of being in a drive-by, especially not in L.A., but when Dice pulled up inches away from the driver seat of Peewee's Towncar, I stuck my thirty-three round tech .9 out of the window and started blasting. All I remembered seeing was blood squirting out of the car and onto my face. Keisha started screaming. She was in the driver seat.

I didn't see or know if I got Shondella, so I slid my hoodie over my head and hopped out of the van. I ran to the passenger side and she was hit in the chest, but still breathing. She looked me in the eyes and said, "I hate you."

I smiled and yelled, "Die bitch!" before I emptied the rest of my clip on her.

I ran back to the van after the shooting and Dice smashed off. I didn't have any remorse afterwards. However, I did hate the fact that Paul was going to grow up parentless because his mother and I couldn't get over our foolishness.

Two hours later, after Dice and I had burned the van and gotten rid of all the evidence, I sat in apartment #10 feeling guilty about my whole life. I glanced at Dice and he was sipping on a bottle of Cognac. The next thing I know, he passed me the bottle. We passed it back and forth all night, reminiscing about the good ol' days. We talked about times we had shared together and with the whole team. We talked about Bull. We talked about Bunch, and we cried when we talked about Peewee and Maine.

By sunrise, we were drunk as two sailors leaving a free Tequila party. The alcohol had taken away all my pain. I fell asleep on cloud nine on the living room floor.

The alcohol had me thinking my life was all good and peaches and cream. I had found a way to escape reality. Cognac was my new friend.

Chapter 19

Daphne

I'd been staying with Jessica for the past two months. Life had been going by in slow motion like a film. It was like a roller coaster. Charlie and I had tested positive for HIV. He'd been MIA since I'd given birth to our son. I saw Charlie once at Peewee's funeral, but when he walked over to me, I knew he was drunk.

He sobbed, "Daphne, I'm sorry! Daphne, I'm sorry!"

I shook my head disgusted. "Charles, I know you're going through a rough time right now, and I also saw the news about Keisha and Shondella, but you need to get yo' shit together! I'm going through it too, but you don't see me walkin' around here all drunk and shit.

Nigga, I got HIV! Do you even know how many nights I have cried myself to sleep and thought about killin' myself?"

Tears rolled down my cheek in rivers. Charlie was so drunk, he just shrugged like he didn't care. I sobbed, "Charles, life is hard as hell on me! I don't have ANYBODY! All I got is the twins and our son! Jessica and Momma can only do so much."

Motherhood was getting the best of me. I was sixteen, but I was living life as if I was twenty-five. Charlie had become a wino. I was losing support from him by the day. It was as if something in his head had just popped and he had lost a few screws.

As they lowered Peewee's body into the ground, I glanced over to where Dice and Zoe stood. Dice was leaning on Zoe's shoulder, crying.

I left Charlie where he stood and walked over to Dice. I called him by his first name and told him, "I need some help!"

"Daphne, I already know," he replied. "Ma, Choo is going through it right now! He believes everything is his fault. His test came back positive, so that's a big dilemma to him. He's—"

I cut Dice off. In a confidential whisper, I said, "I got it too!"

Dice shook his head. "I know. But Daph, as a strong black woman, you gotta understand that some people take things harder than others. Plus, Charlie's conscience is killin' him. He's takin' the blame for the deaths of JR, Peewee, and Bunch. He says it's his fault you have HIV. He takes the blame for Maine and Bull being locked up and lookin' at 100 years. He also takes the responsibility of being a deadbeat father.

"Daph, I'm not makin' an excuse for the man, but Charlie is going through it! This don't justify the way he have been givin' up on life and turnin' to the bottle to escape reality, but truth be told, I was the one who introduced him to the liquid crack."

I looked at Dice and gave him the evil eye. I couldn't believe he was just sitting back watching Charlie give his life up to the bottle. I felt everyone at that funeral was stuck on stupid. I jumped in my Lexus and smashed off.

Two months later, here I was sitting in Jessica's living room watching the twins play with their cousins while I fed Charles. Miss Warner and Jessica were out handling

Charlie's goings on. Charlie had given up on life completely, but I couldn't just let him throw away his life. Just because we were infected with the virus, that didn't mean we had nothing to live for. If nothing else, we had kids who needed our tender loving care.

I was tired of being alone. I needed Charlie by my side. I needed help with the kids. Charlie needed to be at home. I decided to reach out to Dice for support one last time.

He and Zoe had moved to North Carolina. I called him and he answered on the third ring. "Hello!"

"Dice, I'm about to take my gun and go get my husband. And if he don't wanna come, I'ma shoot him."

Dice tried to protest "Naw, Daph, wait 'til I come back down there. I'll be in L.A. two weeks from now."

Without another word, I hung up in Dice's face. It was my job to go get my man, and I wasn't about to let Dice try to talk me out of it. If anything, I didn't need an explanation; I just wanted to be heard. I just wanted someone to hear my cry. I just wanted some understanding.

Chapter 20

Charlie

Ever since the first night Dice and I had gotten drunk, I'd been turning up the bottle. I was trying to escape reality and life all together. Truth be told, I felt like my father and EJ; I couldn't live without the bottle. I even became fond of Chocolate, Joyce, and Mo'nique again. They were the ones who supplied me with the drink. I stayed hiding from life in apartment #10, so I sent one of them to the store for me every day.

I even forgave Joyce for lying to me. She eventually admitted to me that she was messing with three other men that she met at the club. After sitting up thinking about how Lajoi wasn't my daughter, I started thinking about my kids.

I was neglecting my kids. I was neglecting Charlena. I was neglecting Charnay, and I was neglecting my fiancé and Charles JR. I had left Daphne to take care of two kids that weren't even hers.

I was sipping on a bottle of Jack Daniels when reality hit. I slammed it down on my glass table and it shattered the glass. I was drunk, but enough was enough!

I had a visual of my father and EJ, they were sitting next to each other at a bar saying, "Welcome to the club."

I jumped out of that visual real fast. I was sweating, and now having hot flashes. My brother and Peewee then popped in my head.

"The man who wanted me to change done gave up on life himself," Peewee shot. "Cuzz, wake yo' ass up befo' it's too late! You feel me, kid. Money! B! Ock!"

My brother started laughing at Peewee. "Little Eric, you still the same, I see."

Peewee nodded and they hugged. It looked like they were having fun up in heaven. Then my brother got serious.

"Choo, you're letting me down! You saying fuck my kids, fuck your kids, and fuck everything I taught you! As your guardian angel, all I can say is death is lurking. Stop while you're ahead. Love you."

"Yeah, we love you, but don't come join dis club. Not just yet."

They were gone within a blink of an eye. God was trying to get me on the right track. I got up and decided to go home, but the devil was at work and wouldn't let me go home.

There was a sudden knock at the door. It was Mo'nique. "Damn!" I blurted to myself as I opened the door. She had been coming to see me and was my personal bartender for the last two months. There was still a possibility of me being the father of her son, so she started fleecing me.

She used the baby to pry $50,000 out of my hands within one month. In my drunken state of mind, she seemed to always get over on me; especially when she threatened to tell Daphne about the possibility of me being the father of her son.

As I opened the door, she grabbed my crotch and said, "Give me some!"

I snapped. "Bitch, get yo' conniving-ass away from me. You know I'm engaged to your best friend! And let go of my dick! I got AIDS fuckin' with one of you hoes."

I wanted my life back, but females like Mo'nique weren't trying to let me go that easy. They loved my money, not me, and they would have kissed a dog's dick to stay in my pocket.

I slapped her grip from my dick, and she smacked her lips.

"Well, since you act like you don't want me to touch you, I guess I'll go have a talk with my best friend. But, I was coming to tell you, if you give me a quarter million and some dick, I'll leave you alone. Plus, Maine wants me to move to Philly, so I can be close to him."

I replayed the ultimatum over in my head. I wanted to get her out my way, but I'd already learned. I wasn't sticking my dick inside her again.

I told her, "Yo, I'm cool! I got HIV! And I'm not tryna give it to you or nobody else."

Mo'nique was persistent, and I couldn't avoid the temptation that had arisen. Truth be told, I wanted to fuck the shit out of Mo'nique one last time, and tell the bitch to get her triflin'-ass on. In addition, Mo'nique was a freak and loved to get fucked in the ass. Sodomy was a crime to Daphne, and I fell weak to temptation.

"Fuck it! Come on. Let me get a condom."

Chapter 21

Daphne

When Miss Warner and Jessica arrived home, I left the kids with them and headed straight out of the door to Hawthorne. I was going to get Charlie. I was tired of being alone. I was tired of him not taking care of his responsibilities. He needed to be home, and he needed me to help him with his problems. I had to be the grown-up in the relationship. I had to be the bigger person. I had to go put my foot down.

I left Jessica's house and went straight to Sherman Oaks. When I arrived at my house, mail was all over the floor. I stepped right over the mail and walked directly to my closet. I grabbed my .9mm, locked the house back up, and drove to Hawthorne.

It only took thirty minutes to drive through a few cities to get to Hawthorne. I was flying like a bat out of hell in my Lexus. When I arrived, I put the gun in my purse and hopped out.

The apartment complex looked the same from the outside. When I got to the back of the complex, Chocolate was coming out of her apartment.

"Where he at?" I hissed in a high-pitched tone.

"Who?" Chocolate countered.

"Bitch, don't play with me. You know who I'm talkin' bout. Where he at?"

Chocolate must have thought I was playing because she rolled her eyes and said, "That's none of your business."

I pulled out my gun and yelled, "Bitch, I asked you, where he at?"

"If it's dat serious, he's upstairs. And I think Mo'nique up there with him"

Scandalous bitch! I thought as I ran upstairs. I completely blew a fuse when I heard my supposed to be best friend moaning and telling Charlie to fuck her harder. It sounded like they were having sex right behind the door.

I blanked out when I tried to open the door and it was locked. I did some 007 type of shit and shot the door open. Everything else happened in a fog. Charlie was fucking Mo'nique on the pullout bed in the living room. She was on top of him riding his dick like there was no tomorrow. She instantly hopped off him, grabbed her pants, and ran out the door. I wanted to grab her by the weave and beat the living day lights out of her, but I wanted to smash Charlie first.

As he reached for his pants, I pointed my gun and yelled, "I hate you!"

I had nothing to lose. I forgot all about my son and the twins. I forgot about everything we had going for ourselves. The only thing I knew was that my nightmare was becoming reality.

I shot Charlie three times in the back. The impact of the slugs sent him flying to the floor.

I shot three more times, but missed all three shots. By the grace of God, he was lucky, because I don't know how I missed him.

I snapped out of my trance and realized what I'd done. Tears rushed to my eyes and down my cheeks. Charlie was lying on the floor, not moving.

"What have I done?" I asked myself. "I killed my first love. My baby daddy. My fiancé. And my life."

I cried for at least five minutes. I didn't know what to do. Then, all of a sudden, I heard the ghetto bird hovering over the apartment.

I heard LAPD approaching on walkie-talkies, and I heard Mo'nique yelling, "She's upstairs! She got like three to four guns! My baby daddy is a hostage! I think she shot him!"

Mo'nique was straight up shiesty.

LAPD replied, "Okay, get back! We got SWAT on the way."

Just as I heard all the commotion downstairs, Charlie said, "Daph, I can't feel my feet." *He was still alive!* "Ma, you caught me. I apologize. I didn't want to do it... But, shawty, listen to me... Go board up. Lock the doors. I might not make it, so I need you alive. The SWAT team will kill you. Board up and call Jessica."

I jumped up and did exactly as told. I was glad I only had to shoot out one deadbolt on the screen door. I locked the other lock on the door and had Jessica on the phone within minutes. I told her everything and she was immediately on the way.

"Daphne, make sure he don't die!" she cried. "And make sure all the blinds are closed. I will be there in a few minutes."

Jessica hung up and I panicked. "God, please don't let my fiancé die. I don't know what to do."

Charlie was laid out on his belly. He couldn't move. I'd paralyzed him. A bullet had hit his spine. Blood was all over the bed and couch. I just knew he was going to die if I didn't do something.

I sat next to him with the gun I shot him with in my hand. When I realized I was still holding the gun, I tossed it to the other side of the room.

It went off again! I was so gone and distraught, I forgot that it was dangerous to toss a loaded gun.

The police started yelling, "Shots fired! Shots fired!"

Then, I heard a voice say, "Come out with your hands up! Daphne Johnson, the apartment is surrounded."

The next thing I know, Charlie started coughing up blood and the phone rang. I didn't know if I should answer the phone or attend to Charlie.

I panicked again. "God, what am I to do now?"

"Go get the phone," Charlie said as he laid on his face coughing up blood.

I answered the phone. It was Jessica with Jay Cooper on her conference line. The SWAT sergeant was also on the line.

Jessica said, "Daph, I'm outside. Is my brotha still alive?"

I sobbed, "Yes. But he's now coughing up blood, and he told me he can't move."

Jay Cooper chimed in. "Daph, look, everything happened in the heat of passion. You weren't mentally fit, so surrender right now before Charlie dies."

"Okay, okay! I'm bout ta come out with my hands up," I said. "But Sergeant, tell the other officers don't shoot."

Eventually, I surrendered. But before I did, I hung up, ran over to Charlie, gave him a kiss, said a quick prayer, and apologized.

"Charlie, I'm sorry. Please forgive me. I didn't mean to hurt you. I just snapped. Charlie, I love you. Please don't die…"

Chapter 22

Charlie

April 3, 2002

It's been two long years since my baby momma and wife confined me to a wheelchair. I'd played with fire and got burnt. However, mistakes are made, so I forgave Daphne just as she'd forgiven me.

Over the past couple of years, things have changed. Daphne and I jumped the broom. I asked the judge before her trial if he could pronounce us man and wife. I didn't press charges against my wife, but Chocolate and Mo'nique turned state evidence against her. I know they did it because they couldn't stand the fact the Daphne was my main broad. Believe it or not, they even tried to convince me to turn state evidence against Daphne. They came to my bedside at the hospital and swore Daphne wasn't shit and needed to spend the rest of her life behind bars for what she did.

However, to my surprise, Charlene, Jessica, Momma, and Black Dice all decided to side with Daphne. They knew she loved me and that I'd brought my misfortunes on myself. Charlene even went as far as telling Chocolate that a real woman knows when to support the father of her child, especially in a time of need.

Chocolate countered, "Yeah whateva." She didn't know Charlene from jack. Charlene was a fighter. She was a classy broad, but had hands like Laila Ali. She grabbed Chocolate by the weave and slammed her face first into a glass window. Chocolate tried to defend herself but she was no match for Charlene.

As Charlene beat Chocolate half to death, she taunted, "Bitch, I'm from the derty, we get down. You can't see me." Charlene grew up in the Bankhead Projects, so she'd had her fair share of fights. She carried herself very well, so you would have never figured she had a wild side.

After the incident, Chocolate and Mo'nique started working with the people to the extreme. They tried to get me indicted on charges of drug trafficking. They told the people everything they knew about me and my empire. Good thing they didn't know too much about me, but what I led them to believe. And the shit they knew was the shit they were mostly involved in, so the case they tried to build wasn't nothing but a bunch of he-say she-say.

Luckily, Dice and I had turned legit right before our empire crumbled. And come to find out, if it wasn't for the alcohol in my system, I would have bled to death. For the first time in my life, alcohol did good to me. Jack Daniels saved my life.

Maria is currently serving a 5 year bid. She's incarcerated for burglary after trying to break into someone's house to support her crack habit. Gotti B and Ralph tried their best to get her to kick the habit, but crack was her master. Bi-weekly, Gotti or Sheena take $100 and put it on Maria's books. They're married too. Black Dice and Zoe have also jumped the bloom. Dice has a junior, and Zoe is pregnant again, so Dice gets pussy after all...

Daphne was sixteen when she shot me. She's eighteen now, and will be nineteen in a couple of months. Today, she's being released from jail, and I can't wait to see her. The family and I are headed to pick her up. We're in a stretch limo, about to bring my wife home in style. I went to pick up her parents so we could all rekindle our relationships. Life is too short. I have to man up. Daphne needs her parents, so I begged them to ride with me and my family to pick her up from prison.

Our son, Charles JR is two, going on three; I am so glad he gets to see his grandparents. Somehow, once again, Jessica managed to do magic. Inside this limo, my whole blood line is present, except my daughter by Chocolate. Ever since she and Mo'nique turned state evidence against Daphne, they'd been MIA. I think she and Joyce went back home to Spokane, Washington. Word on the streets is that Mo'nique jumped state with them, because in the projects she was labeled a snitch.

Her sister finally came out of the closet. I saw her the other day in traffic, and she looked like Little Bow Wow in drag.

Also, as a man living with HIV, I now travel around the world telling my story. I travel from state to state like

I did when I was moving weight, but now it's for a positive cause. HIV is at an all-time high. Black folks have the highest percentage of new cases, so if you play with fire, you will get burnt! Word to the wise, protect yourself.

Black Dice is now, one of the leading investors on Wall Street. In a year or two, he'll probably become a member of the billionaire boys club. Maine and Bull are cellmates in a federal prison in Pennsylvania. They both received over 100 years. Ralph and Big Booty Judy just had a baby, but their relationship is on and off. Tracy is still running around Philly with her head cut off. I feel sorry for her and her son.

Most notably, I'm still helping Shodella's mother take care of Paul. Even though I look at him a little differently because he's not my biological son, it bothers me that I killed his mother.

Hey! What can I say? Life goes on.

Chapter 23

Daphne

April 3, 2002

I'm still sitting here waiting to be released from LA. County Jail. I've been waiting for at least six hours. I'm so anxious to get out and see my family, I'm now pacing the whole cell back and forth. I'm so eager to be released, but I hope you, the reader has learned something from my story. Life is precious, and if you don't be careful, you could be living a nightmare!

Remember this…

One can only fight for something that one loves.

One can only love what one respects.

In order to respect anything or anyone, one must at least have some knowledge of oneself!

Peace,

Daphne

No Brakes Publishing Order Form

Title	Quantity	Price	Total
Boy I Had Enough		$15.00	
Southside King		$15.00	
Ratchet Ville – Vol 1-3		$15.00	
To Live and Die in LA		$15.00	
Natural Born Killaz		$15.00	
Girl I Had Enough		$15.00	

Shipping and Handling $5.60

Name: ______________________________

Address: ____________________________

City: ____________ State: _______ Zip Code: _______

Email: ______________________________

Mail order form along with money order for payment to:

No Brakes Publishing

Attn: Author Terry Wroten

7324 Crenshaw #10

Los Angeles, CA 90043

Also available from No Brakes Publishing

Natural Born Killaz

To Live & Die in LA

Girl, I Had Enough

Molly

Ratchet Ville

Ratchet Ville 2

Ratchet Ville 3

Corporate Thuggin'

Good Girl Gone Bad

Ghetto Diva

Southside King

ANTHOLOGY

The Massacre